THE AFTERLIFE OF SLIM McCORD

Rogues Blackman and Tanner have seen it all, but nothing has prepared them for what they find in the town of Possum Creek: the preserved corpse of their long-ago compadre, the outlaw Slim McCord, being exhibited in a travelling carny show! Outraged, the pair decide to steal him away and give his mortal remains a decent burial. But before he is laid to rest, Slim will take part in one last bank job alongside his old friends . . .

JACK MARTIN

THE AFTERLIFE OF SLIM McCORD

Complete and Unabridged

LINFORD
Leicester

First published in Great Britain in 2013 by
Robert Hale Limited
London

First Linford Edition
published 2015
by arrangement with
Robert Hale Limited
London

A catalogue record for this book is available
from the British Library.

ISBN 978–1–4448–2537–4

Published by
F. A. Thorpe (Publishing)
Anstey, Leicestershire

Set by Words & Graphics Ltd.
Anstey, Leicestershire
Printed and bound in Great Britain by
T. J. International Ltd., Padstow, Cornwall

This book is printed on acid-free paper

This one is for Beth

Author's Note

They say that truth is stranger than fiction and although many of the events in this story may seem fantastic, not least of which is a band of desperados riding around with a mummified outlaw, I would point you to the strange story of Elmer McCurdy, a real-life outlaw who was indeed mummified.

In 1911 McCurdy was shot during a failed robbery and, as no one claimed his body, the undertaker embalmed the outlaw with an arsenic-based preservative and put the corpse on display. From there the corpse ended up in various travelling shows before disappearing sometime in the 1930s. Incredibly in 1976, a prop man on the set of the TV series, *The Six Million Dollar Man*, rediscovered it. It had been thought to be a wax model, and used in a fun house set before a finger broke off, revealing it to be actual human remains.

Elmer McCurdy was eventually buried in 1977 in the Boot Hill section of Summit View Cemetery, Oklahoma with most of the cast and crew from *The Six Million Dollar Man* in attendance.

This book is also dedicated to the memory of Elmer McCurdy and all those who rode the Wild West, both in life and death.

1

'Shot in the back,' the barker yelled. 'Ain't no lawman who could have taken Mad Slim McCord face on.'

'You sure got that right.' Clay Blackman offered a nickel but the barker held up his hands, palms forward.

'No, no, old-timer.' He shook his head vigorously. 'Not me, give it to him.'

'Him?'

'Sure,' the barker smiled. 'Put it in his mouth. He's the one you're paying to see and it's only right he takes your money.'

'In his mouth?'

'Sure, he'll gobble it right up.'

Blackman frowned. It seemed a particularly gruesome thing to do but nevertheless he pushed the coin between his dead friend's lips. He winced as his fingers brushed the dry, almost abrasive tongue.

Strange but McCord didn't even look dead, propped up as he was against a wooden frame, more like he was sleeping on his feet. The preservation was incredible, and the dead man's skin, although cold and leathery, seemed to glow with vigour. His eyes of course were glass; Blackman knew that because Slim's eyes had been a pale grey, rather than the vibrant blue that now stared sightlessly into an unfocused distance. One of the eyes had also been placed at an irregular angle, which gave Slim something of a cock-eyed appearance.

'How'd he end up like this?' Blackman wasn't aware that he had given the thought a voice.

'Well now.' The barker rubbed his chin, as though considering his reply rather than going into a well-practised sales pitch. 'Was a time Mad Slim McCord was one of the most feared men in the West. He terrorized the badlands and sent many a lawman to an early grave.'

Blackman smiled at that. As far as he knew Slim had never been much of a killer; he hadn't liked killing, and would avoid doing so whenever it was possible. He tended to scare folks with a dazzling combination of skilful gunplay, which was often all it took. One time, Blackman remembered, Slim had shot a sheriff's hat clean off his head and then plugged it twice more as it spun through the air. After that the lawman hadn't been any trouble to them and they had been free to go about their unlawful business.

'The fact that he lived as long as he did is testament to how successful a bandit he was,' the barker continued. 'But McCord's luck ran out one day down in Santino when a lawman recognized him from an old Wanted poster and shot him in the back. Just like that. No warning and a bullet in the back.'

'Long way from Santino,' Blackman said. 'How'd he end up here?'

'You see, no one claimed the body,'

the barker said. 'And so the undertaker, figuring he could profit from such an infamous outlaw, decided to embalm the body in preserving solution made of arsenic and strong spirits.'

'And you bought him?' Blackman looked the barker directly in the eyes.

The barker nodded, proudly.

'He's been dead close on seven years now and looks as if he could have been shot this very morning,' the barker said. 'The undertaker had to remove a lot of his innards you know, stuff him back up with sawdust and the like, but that's a darn fine preservation job, darn fine. American craftsmanship at its best.'

'You bought the body to turn a profit?' Blackman found that the most tasteless thing he had ever heard.

'Sure did,' the barker said. 'And I charge a nickel a view. That's what's called the entrepreneurial spirit operating in a free market. God bless America.'

'Guess he sure ain't gonna choke on that nickel,' Blackman said.

'We're only here one week in Possum Creek,' the barker said with a broad smile. 'Be sure to tell all your friends.'

Immediately another man entered, holding his nickel out between a thumb and forefinger. There was a queue of at least fifty people outside the tent waiting for a chance to see the dead man.

Slim had never been that successful an outlaw, Blackman recalled, and guessed that he was making more money dead than he ever had alive.

'I hear he's been preserved with a paint made of strong whiskey,' someone in the crowd said, as Blackman pushed through and made his way to the saloon.

⋆　⋆　⋆

'Ghoulish,' Blackman said. 'That's what it is, ghoulish.'

'Sure don't seem right.' Tanner drained his glass and immediately slid it across the counter to the barkeep. 'Put

5

another whiskey in there.'

Two cowmen, still dusty from the trail, came in and took up positions next to Blackman and Tanner at the bar. They both tipped their hats in greeting and then bunched together, losing themselves in their own concerns.

'Don't seem right because it ain't right,' Blackman said, and then went on to repeat himself. 'Ghoulish is what it is.'

'Gives me the spooks to just think about it,' Tanner agreed.

The two men fell silent while they drank, both lost in private but common thoughts of the many years they had spent riding with Slim McCord. Those years may have often been hard, but, as the two men looked back, they were imbued with a rosy glow. Forgotten were all the times when they'd had to bed down on the hard ground, more often than not freezing because they couldn't light a fire else they alert some passing law, or the many many times they'd ridden with empty bellies and pockets that didn't stretch to a meal. Instead, they saw their past as a golden place — an El Dorado in the sun, and Slim McCord had been a big part of those golden years.

They had been young men when they'd first ridden together and although neither of them could remember exactly how long ago it was since they'd first taken the owlhoot trail, they knew it had been a mighty long time ago. It had been well before the war. They were both in their late-sixties, so it was a good guess that they had first met a stretch more than forty years ago.

'Do you recall when we first met him?' Blackman asked, presently. 'I can still see those two naked women if I close my eyes.'

Tanner laughed at that. If he thought real hard, pushed through the sands time had scattered over the memory, then he too could see them.

'To think,' he said, 'that the bestest and bravest man a fella's ever had the pleasure to ride with should end up being part of a travelling carny show.'

'Yeah.' Blackman shook his head and drained his own glass. He motioned for the barkeep to leave the bottle and then poured himself another drink. 'Usually the deal is when you die you get to rest, but poor old Slim's still on the move. That barker's doing a roaring trade with our pard's mortal remains.'

'Ain't right.'

'Nope.' Blackman had by this point drained and filled his glass twice more, and was starting to feel that fuzzy glow above his eyes. 'It's as wrong as wrong can be.'

★ ★ ★

Yesteryear

Blackman and Tanner were still giggling when the stranger came up silently behind them and cocked his big old Colt Paterson. Their hilarity ceased just as soon as they heard that hammer go back, and they looked at each other and then turned to look into the face of a grinning gunman. At first they didn't make out any of the man's features as their attention was solidly focused on the cold mouth of the iron the man held in his hand.

'Slide your guns from leather,' the gunman said. 'Nice and slowly and toss them on the ground.'

Blackman and Tanner both did so.

'Good, now sit down on the ground.'

Again Blackman and Tanner obeyed and the gunman went and scooped up their guns and slid them into his own gunbelt. Only then did he seem to relax and although he kept his weapon trained on them he was visibly more at ease.

'Let's see what amused you two.' The gunman walked around them and looked down over the banking to the river below. He saw the two women, naked, bathing in the clear mountain waters.

'We weren't doing no harm,' Tanner said, but was silenced when Blackman elbowed him in the ribs.

The gunman turned back and looked at Blackman and Tanner.

'You know these ladies?' he asked.

'Nope,' Blackman said. 'We just came upon them.'

'We weren't gonna hurt them none,' Tanner said. 'Just looking is all. You can't blame a man for that.'

'Well I don't blame you.' The gunman smiled. 'They sure are a pair of fine looking ladies.'

It was a glorious afternoon and other than the giggles of the two women in the river and the gentle hum of the breeze through the trees, all was silent. The gunman watched the women some more and then turned back to the two men.

'Where you heading?' he asked, but before he could get an answer from either of the men the roar of gunfire filled the air. This was closely followed by screams of alarm from the two women in the river. The gunman looked back towards the women and saw three men, each of them holding iron, standing at the river's edge. They were laughing and motioning for the women to forget their modesty and get out of the water.

'Those fellas with you?' the gunman asked.

'No, sir,' Blackman said, and despite the fact that he was unarmed, he crawled forward and lay on the ground next to the gunman. Tanner waited a moment as if to see what would happen to his pard and then he too crawled towards the edge of the bank.

'We thought we were all alone out here,' Tanner said, looking directly at the man with the gun. 'Then first we come across those women, then you turn up and now this.'

'It sure is getting mighty crowded out here,' the gunman said. Then: 'Are you sure you aren't nothing to do with those excitable fellas down there?'

Both Tanner and Blackman shook their heads.

'If you're joshing me I'll kill you,' the

gunman said and slid the men's weapons from his gunbelt and placed them on the ground. He kept his Colt in his hand but no longer pointed it at the two men. 'The way I see it is those fellas down there are a bad sort and you may need these.'

Blackman and Tanner exchanged glances, but at first made no move to take their weapons.

'Name's Samuel Isaacs McCord. Friends call me Slim.'

'Clay Blackman,' Blackman said, and carefully took his gun. He didn't want to spook this man McCord with any sudden moves.

'Tanner,' Tanner said, and that was all the name he had ever needed. He took his own weapon.

The three men crouched looking down over the bank and Slim flinched when one of the men below fired into the river, ordering the women, who were both holding their arms in such a way as to cover their breasts, out of the water and on to dry land. The women were shaking their heads and pleading with the three men to be left alone, but that wasn't going to happen and the men were all laughing and shouting out crude remarks.

The way Slim saw it the men must have been aware of the women's presence and had managed to sneak up on them, maybe they had even been following them for some ways. It wouldn't have been too difficult to take the women by surprise and he guessed the men must have tied up their horses somewhere in the scrub and gone to the river on foot. There were two mules, no doubt belonging to the women, chewing on the foliage at the river's edge. The dumb beasts were not startled by the men and continued with their foraging, ignoring everything going on around them. One of the mules had a battered Stetson upon its head, holes cut into the brim through which its ears protruded.

'This is gonna get nasty,' Slim said. 'Those fellas down there mean to take those women for their own pleasure.'

'Sure seems that way,' Blackman agreed.

'They'll likely kill them afterwards,' Tanner pointed out. He had heard tell of men like this and didn't much like the stories he had been told.

'And we gotta stop them.' Slim looked at Blackman and Tanner. 'You two with me on this?'

Blackman and Tanner exchanged a glance and then nodded.

'We're with you,' Blackman said.

'Then the way I see it . . . ' Slim looked around them and then back at the men below. One of the women was cautiously wading over to the river's edge while one of the men stood on the bank, arm out, eagerly awaiting her. 'Those men don't know how many guns we have up here. I want you two to spread out while I go down and shake them up some. Don't fire until I give the signal and when I do I want you to fire off a few rounds, but move about between shots. Likely I can bluff these men that there's a bunch of guns with me.'

'What's the signal?' Blackman asked.

Slim looked at him, smiled, and ran a hand through the stubble on his chin.

'I'm gonna get as close as I can,' he said. 'I'll maybe get to the bottom of this slope before they notice me since they seem to be concentrating on the women. And I'll fire a warning shot, but when I fire for the second time I want you two to open up.'

'Got it.' Blackman slid over to the far left of the slope, while Tanner went in the opposite direction.

Slim stood up, looked towards the heavens, crossed himself and then slowly started down the bank.

Below him the woman had reached the river's edge but was still reluctant to get out of the water. She pointed to her clothes, but the men were laughing and then one of them picked up the clothes the women had arranged neatly on a large rock and started dancing about. The other woman remained in the water, watching her companion. Even from this distance Slim could see the fear in her face.

Slim reached the foot of the bank without the men noticing him. He now stood less than twenty feet from the men and, just as the man grabbed the woman's hand and was about to pull her naked from the water, he let off a warning shot, firing into the ground at the dancing man's feet, sending dirt spitting into the air.

The three men suddenly forgot the woman and turned to face Slim.

Slim smiled.

'Howdy, boys,' he said.

The men exchanged puzzled looks and then one of them, a tall gangly-looking man with long black hair that framed the cruel lines of his face, stepped forward and regarded Slim through eyes that were hooded like those of a hawk.

'You figuring on taking on the three of us?' he asked.

'Could be,' Slim said. 'If you fellas

push it that way.'

'If we push it that way!' The man looked at Slim, a mixture of amazement and perhaps fear in his eyes.

Slim nodded. 'Though to be honest,' he said, 'I would rather the three of you rode away nice and peaceable. But if you push it then I'll kill you.'

'You sound mighty confident.' The man spat into the dust.

'I am that,' Slim said.

'One gun against three don't seem like good odds,' the man said. 'Least not from your side. Looks to me like the cards are stacked in my favour.'

'You ain't seen my hand,' Slim said and raised his gun and fired into the air. Almost immediately a barrage of gunfire followed from the bank above. Slim smiled, counting over seven shots before there was silence.

The two gunmen furthest away were visibly shaken and were looking to the third man for guidance.

'You want to play your hand now?' Slim asked, a smile upon his face and the hint of laughter in his pale grey eyes.

For a moment it seemed as if the man was indeed ready to answer the gunfire and Slim tensed, but then the man slid his gun back into its leather and backed away to the other two men who followed his lead and holstered their weapons.

'I see you again, I'll kill you, stranger,' the man said.

'Sure,' Slim smiled again. 'I'll likely manage to avoid such an ugly three-some as you fellas.'

'You do that,' the man said, and then once more spat into the dirt. He started walking along the trail, his men following behind. Slim waited until they were out of sight before collecting together the women's clothes and placing them on the river's edge.

'I'll turn my back,' he said, 'while you ladies climb out and get dressed.'

'Thank you,' one of the women said.

Slim turned away and looked up the

hill, wondering if Blackman and Tanner were getting an eyeful as the women climbed from the river behind him.

2

Night had fallen long before Blackman and Tanner left the saloon and stepped on to the dusty street. Neither of them was exactly sure what time it was, but they knew it must be late because the saloon had been winding down for the night, and the street was virtually deserted. Back in the day the town would have remained rowdy throughout the night and into the early hours, but the railroad had put an end to all that. The town of Possum Creek was no longer besieged by trail thirsty cowboys and had become respectable.

Blackman swallowed a huge lungful of the cool night air and smiled to himself. The West, he thought was growing old and tired, as was he. Nothing was like it used to be and pretty soon the frontier, what little was left of it, would be gone. Progress they called it and

Blackman guessed that at least some of what he saw around him was a progression of sorts, but at the same time there was much to be said for the old ways, much that had gone forever and would be sorely missed. He didn't much like the modern world and was glad that he wouldn't be around to see a heck of a lot more of it.

'You shay . . .' Blackman said, but his words trailed off when he realized he was a little too drunk to talk.

Tanner, finding himself in a similar predicament, simply grunted his agreement. Not that he had any idea what his friend had been trying to say, but figured it didn't really matter as he was too drunk to understand it even if it had been intelligible.

The two men walked on a-ways, stumbling about in a drunken, ill-coordinated fashion. At one point Tanner began to go sideways like a crab and then circled Blackman before pitching forward into a picket fence that had been constructed around the town bank. It was at that point that the two men decided they needed to sit down and they both lowered themselves to the dirt and sat with their backs to the fence.

Blackman looked back over his shoulder at the bank, recollecting that he'd robbed a few of those in his time. He smiled, knowing that this here bank was perfectly safe and that he was far too old to pose a threat to the money snuggled away inside, but all the same it was nice to think about doing it again and he turned to talk to Tanner but saw that his friend was fast asleep, his chin buried in his chest.

'Damn!' Blackman said.

He knew that he should try and get Tanner to his feet and lead him back to the rooms they had paid for, but he doubted he'd be able to wake him and even if he did it was a long walk back to the hotel. Far too long a walk in his drunken condition when all he wanted to do was sleep off the whiskey, sleep and dream of robbing banks, kissing ladies and riding across miles and miles of utter freedom. Those days were gone though and Blackman knew it. It was written in his face and he had a wrinkle for every fence that had been thrown up around previously open range. He could dream though, and in his dreams there were no fences, and enough pretty ladies to warm the coldest of nights. Within minutes Blackman too had succumbed to the intoxication and was happily snoring away as he rode the dreamscape ranges of memory.

The two ageing men, one-time outlaws, lifelong friends, sat there side by side and slept beneath the stars, just as they had so many times before. The drink inside them insulated their bones from the chill of the night and the ground beneath them felt as comfortable as the softest of beds. And, although neither of them was aware of it, they had collapsed directly opposite the carny tent that contained their dead friend's remains.

*   ★   ★

'Excuse me, gentlemen.'

Blackman opened his eyes and immediately wished he hadn't when the daylight seemed to sear into his brain. It took him a moment to focus, but when he did he found himself looking up into the face of a beautiful young woman.

He felt Tanner leaning against him and nudged him awake.

'Are you OK?' the woman asked.

'We're fine, ma'am,' Blackman said. 'Guess we must have overdid the old firewater last night.'

Tanner looked first at the woman and then at his friend. He rubbed his eyes with the backs of his hands, feeling lousy.

The woman was standing over them, a brown package held beneath one arm and a small umbrella in the other. She smiled but there was a look in her eyes that seemed to say, *You two are a little old for this kind of behaviour.*

24

'If you'll excuse me,' she said and opened the gate in the middle of the fence and walked up to the bank. She took a key from a chain she wore around her neck and, after glancing back at the two old men, let herself in.

Blackman took his makings from his pocket and made himself a quirly.

'We've slept here all night?'

'Yep.'

Blackman lit his smoke and handed his makings to his friend.

'He's in there,' Blackman said, pointing to the carny tent across the street.

'Uh?' Tanner looked up.

'There,' Blackman pointed. 'Slim's in there.'

Tanner nodded, said nothing, and tried to work a kink out of his neck. He didn't think there was a square inch of his body that wasn't aching. He was just too darned old for sleeping in the street like this. He looked across the street and even from this distance could read the large writing on the board outside the carny tent: **ONE WEEK AND ONE WEEK ONLY IN POSSUM CREEK.**

'What time do you think it is?' Blackman asked.

Tanner shrugged. The sun was low in the sky and the street was still deserted so he knew it was early, but he had no idea how early. Banks usually opened for business around nine and the woman, likely a secretary, had let herself in with a key so it would seem likely that it wasn't yet nine.

Blackman stood up, groaned and then pulled his friend to his feet.

'Come on,' he said, and made his way across the street to the tent.

They reached it and Blackman fumbled with the strips of rawhide that held the door flaps closed. The flap was tied in several places and it took the man a few minutes before they opened enough for him to go in.

Blackman looked back at his companion and then stepped into the tent. Tanner took another look up and down the street, which was still deserted, before following his friend inside.

Immediately through the doorway they found themselves looking up at Slim.

'See?' Blackman said.

This was the first time Tanner had seen the corpse and he stared open-mouthed at his old friend.

Slim was tied to the wooden frame that acted as a support and was standing upright like some cigar store Indian. He was dressed in a faded pair of pants, a threadbare shirt and around his waist he wore a battered gunbelt. There was no gun in the single rawhide holster that hung from the belt and his general appearance was one of a saddle-tramp, but he did have on a pretty decent pair of boots, even if they were mud stained and heavily worn at the heels. Upon his head sat the same battered old Stetson he'd always worn and arranged in his hands, tied tightly, was a board that proclaimed, **MAD SLIM MCCORD — TERROR OF THE WEST**. There weren't that many other exhibits around them though

Tanner did notice a Comanche lance and a two-headed beaver; the second head, he could see, had been clumsily sewn onto the poor creature.

'He almost looks alive,' Tanner said, marvelling at how well preserved his friend was.

'We should take him,' Blackman said and grabbed the frame that held his friend, testing its weight.

'Where we gonna take him?'

'Anywhere.'

'Why?'

'Because' — Blackman yanked on the frame, pulled the body forward a couple of inches — 'this just ain't right.' He tore the board from his dead friend's hands, snapping the string that held it in position, and tossed it aside.

'But what will we do with him?'

'We could bury him.'

'Where?'

'Anywhere but here. Put him to rest. Slim deserves that.'

'He sure does,' Tanner agreed. 'But we can't just steal his body.'

'Why not?' Blackman put his hands around the centre of the wooden frame and slid it towards the opening in the tent. There wasn't any real weight there and with Tanner's help it would be easy enough to get Slim away. 'Slim had no kin. Hell, I guess we are the closest thing to kin that he ever did know. So if anyone's got the right to see that old Slim gets a decent burial then it is us two old fools.'

Tanner couldn't argue with that.

'I guess so,' he said.

Not believing what they were doing, Tanner reached out and held on to the wooden frame, helping his friend manoeuvre it towards the entrance of the tent.

'We'll cut him loose,' Blackman said, 'tie him on to one of our horses and then bury him a few miles outside of town, maybe up in the mountains, put a marker on the grave and all.'

Tanner nodded, figuring that this was the Christian thing to do. The proper thing to do.

'Slim'd like that,' he said.

Blackman reached into his own belt for his knife, but in the confined space of the tent he lost his footing and found himself pitching forward. The frame supporting the dead outlaw swung widely and Tanner fell backwards, landing heavily on his rump.

Both men cursed and were about to get back to their feet when a curious thing happened. The frame that supported Slim's body had been rocking gently but it suddenly shot forward, crashing against the canvas of the tent, creating a long, jagged rip in the tent wall. Slim, of course, still attached, went with it and came to rest half in and half out of the tent. Most of his body remained inside the tent but his head had gone through the rip and was now outside, the dead eyes staring up at the morning sky.

'Damn.' Blackman got to his feet just as the loudest scream he had ever heard almost burst his eardrums. The scream seemed to grow in power until it became one almighty roar.

'Let's get out of here.' Tanner grabbed Blackman and both men exited the tent by sliding under the canvas at the rear. The street was filling with people so they quickly ran around to the front.

Blackman soon saw the origin of that awful scream — an elderly lady standing next to Slim's body was screaming loud enough to wake the dead. She had her hands up to her face, her eyes bulging in sheer terror, and she stamped her feet on the ground as she stared down at the corpse.

Slim seemed oblivious to this and he continued to stare sightlessly at the sky.

'Come on.' Tanner pulled his friend into the crowd that had formed so they could lose themselves amongst the chaos. There was no point in being arrested for attempted body snatching. The two retreated, and stopped by the bank's picket fence, watching as the carny owner and a man wearing a sheriff's badge made their way through the crowd.

'Looks like Slim's gonna get himself arrested,' Blackman said and Tanner smiled at the grim humour. They noticed the young woman who had spoken to them earlier had come out of the bank, and was standing next to a portly, officious-looking man. It seemed the entire town had turned out to witness the chaos they had caused.

'The body's possessed,' someone shouted, which had the result of making the old woman scream louder still and this time she was joined by several other women attempting to harmonize with her.

'Slim McCord's returned from the grave,' someone else yelled.

Blackman smiled. Slim would have got a kick from this, from knowing that even in death he was capable of whipping up a storm.

'What happened?' Blackman addressed his question to the woman who had spoken to them earlier. He was wide awake now and feeling far bolder than he had in many a sunrise and, although he was long past it in the romance stakes, there was something about the woman's beauty that made him feel far younger than he was.

'I'm not sure,' she said, smiling warmly at both Blackman and Tanner. She looked to her colleague but his attention remained fixed on the commotion opposite.

'Quite a fuss,' Blackman said, giving a wide smile full of tobacco-stained teeth.

'It is that,' the young woman said.

'Come along, Miss Cooper,' the officious-looking man said, casting a distasteful eye at the two old men, as though he had only just noticed their presence. 'We've bank business to attend to.'

Blackman smiled as the man led the woman back into the bank. As he watched them go he noticed a small object fall from the hem of the man's pants. He was about to shout out, but quickly thought better of it. He waited

3

'We ain't as young as we used to be,' Blackman said, twirling the key over and over in his hand, 'but I still reckon there ain't a safe I can't open.'

'You're loco.' Tanner took his makings and quickly put together a smoke. They were sat on the bench outside the saloon, beers in hand. It was comfortable here, not too hot thanks to the shade provided by a tall tree that towered above them.

'That may be so.' Blackman held up the key and smiled. 'But I reckon Slim's behind this.'

'Slim's dead,' Tanner said.

'I know that,' Blackman laughed. 'But maybe he's helping us from the hereafter, looking down at us.'

'That's loco.'

'Is it? It was strange how Slim's body just pitched forward like that, and even stranger how that bank manager, if that's who he was, dropped this here key in the dirt. Those types of fellas are not usually so careless with the keys to the bank.'

'You don't know if it is the bank key,' Tanner pointed out and drew on his smoke.

'Oh, it is,' Blackman said and tossed the key from one hand to another. 'And we're gonna rob that there bank and, what's more, we gonna take Slim's body with us when we leave town. Can you imagine that — Slim coming on another job long after he's dead? That would be a story that would be told forever.'

Tanner looked at his friend and frowned. He knew the man well enough to see that this was no joke and that Blackman meant to do just what he said. They'd been involved in some crazy schemes in their time, but this one seemed like the craziest thing he'd ever heard. Not only were they going to rob a bank again after more than ten years of retirement, but they were adding body-snatching to their crimes.

'I've got it all worked out,' Blackman smiled. 'Every little detail.'

Tanner looked around them and although there were plenty of people in the street that afternoon nobody seemed to be taking any notice of them. They were just two old men enjoying the sun and no one paid them no mind. He looked down the street and saw that there was a long queue waiting outside the carny tent to view Slim's remains. After the commotion this morning the body seemed to have gained a new infamy and it looked as if everyone in town was lining up to see the corpse that wouldn't rest. The industrious carny owner had even changed the boarding outside the tent to read: **SLIM MCCORD — THE REST-LESS OUTLAW**.

'That still ain't right,' Tanner said. 'Slim shouldn't be a part of any freak show.'

'That's reason enough to take him,' Blackman said and swallowed a mouthful of the cool beer.

'I guess so,' Tanner nodded and gulped his own drink. He wiped his mouth on the back of a hand.

'Let's get our horses,' Blackman said. 'We'll take a ride out of town and I'll tell you my plan.'

'After we've gotten ourselves some food in our bellies,' Tanner said and drained his beer. 'I've worked up quite an appetite and I don't much like listening to horse-shit on an empty belly.'

* * *

'So you see,' Blackman said. 'That's how we do it.'

They had ridden several miles out of town and were allowing their horses to graze in the long prairie grasses, while they sat on a rotting tree stump and smoked cigarettes. The sun was high in the sky but not too intense and both men felt comfortable, relaxed.

'As easy as that?' Tanner said and drew on his quirly.

'As easy as that,' Blackman nodded, pleased with himself. Now that he had laid out his plan and was thinking of it in the terms of something they would actually do, he felt younger than he had in a long time. Maybe his best years were behind him but he still had plenty of kick left in his old bones, and he was getting tired of merely drifting from town to town while they waited for what little money they had to run out.

Blackman's plan was quite simple — using the key he had found, they'd let themselves into the bank during the night. Then it would be a matter of opening the safe and Blackman was pretty confident that shouldn't prove a problem since, in his own words, there weren't a safe built that he couldn't crack. Before that they would retrieve Slim's body and, when they rode out of town, they would take him with them. He would be buried further down the trail and they would then disappear with their funds much replenished, and live out the rest of their lives in comfort

39

in the knowledge that their oldest and bestest friend was finally at rest.

'You want to know what I think?' Tanner asked presently.

'Sure,' Blackman said, and stubbed out his smoke on the heel of his boot.

'I think you're a loco redneck peckerwood,' Tanner said; it was an insult he tended to use several times a day. 'Firstly you don't know if that key you found is for the bank, and secondly you don't even know what safe they have in there.'

'The key is for the bank,' Blackman said, removed it from his pocket and regarded it for a moment before popping it back into his pocket. 'And the bank's a modern building so I'm figuring the safe is likely a Baum or a Parker. Maybe even a Bradley, but it don't matter. My ears are still good and I can hear those tumblers give.'

'When you figuring on pulling this off?' Tanner asked.

'Tonight,' Blackman said. 'Don't want to give them time to change the locks on the bank.'

'Loco redneck peckerwood,' Tanner reiterated, his repertoire of insults being rather limited. 'You're gonna get us killed.'

Blackman smiled.

'You're in then?' he asked.

'Ain't got nothing else to do but grow old,' Tanner said, and lay back in the grass. He closed his eyes, figuring that if he was going to be riding through the night then this was as good a time as any to catch up on a little sleep.

★   ★   ★

Yesteryear

'You reckon?' Blackman asked.

'I reckon.' Slim nodded, turning the note over and over in his hand. He looked at the note again — LEAVE TOWN! OR ELSE! BY ORDER OF THE SHERIFF!

Blackman looked at Tanner.

'He reckons,' he said.

'I heard him.'

'Then come on, boys,' Slim said. 'Follow me.'

It was a good five-mile walk back into town, but they managed to keep up a steady pace and the journey took them a little over ninety minutes. The three of them stood together at the town boundary, looking down at the sign that proudly proclaimed, WELCOME TO HOPE SPRINGS.

'Some welcome,' Blackman said, and pulled his makings from a shirt pocket. He rolled himself a quirly and popped it into his mouth.

'We'll find our horses first,' Slim said. 'Get them ready for a quick getaway.'

'What about our guns?' Tanner asked, feeling naked without his rig.

'He's right,' Blackman drew on his quirly. 'Guns seem more important than horses right about now.'

'Guess we'll have to steal a few weapons,' Slim answered, peering at the town in the distance. It shimmered in the heat-haze.

The three men had ridden into town

late yesterday afternoon, their pockets bulging after three months hired on as cowhands at the Lucky Arrow ranch. All they'd wanted was a good meal, a bottle of whiskey each and maybe a card game, give them a chance to turn the money in their pockets into a small fortune. Between them they carried over $800, a sizeable amount of money but the prospect of increasing their stake in a good old game of chance was surely tempting.

And that's just what they'd done. First they checked their horses into the livery stable and then, without bothering to wash the trail dust from them, they had gone into the Liberty saloon and between them consumed three pans of beans and a good helping of succulent bacon. Then they'd started on the whiskey and before they knew it they were sitting in on a poker game with four other fellas who resided in the town. One of the men, a man called Deke, was actually town sheriff and, the three men learned, was more than partial to spending his evenings playing cards, drinking and whoring.

The game had been five-card draw and Slim immediately hit a winning streak. He'd taken a few hundred from the other players, including Blackman and Tanner — though that didn't really matter none as the three men intended to split whatever collective winnings they'd made when they left town. Though as the game progressed, going on well into the night, Slim found himself losing what he'd won, as well as a goodly amount of his own money. He clawed most of it back and was once more winning, as was Blackman who had doubled his original stake, when the sheriff ordered more whiskey from the barkeep, a man he called Rycott, adding that he wanted the good stuff.

And for Slim, Blackman and Tanner the rest of the night was a complete mystery and the next thing they knew they were waking up more than five miles outside of town. Each of them had a blinding headache, not a single cent in their pockets, no gunbelt and no horse. They'd obviously been drugged, something in the whiskey, 'the good stuff', robbed and then hauled out here and dumped during the night. The only clue to what had happened was a note that someone, likely the sheriff, had slipped into Slim's breast pocket.

LEAVE TOWN! OR ELSE! BY ORDER OF THE SHERIFF!

'The livery stable,' Slim said. 'Maybe we can find us a couple of guns there. If not, then at least we'll be able to ensure our horses are still there.'

'What do we do then?' Blackman asked.

Slim smiled.

'We march over to the sheriff's office,' he said. 'And I'll put a gun in his mouth and demand our money. Once we've gotten it we'll leave Hope Springs and never return again.'

'As simple as that?' Tanner said.

'As simple as that.' Slim nodded.

'Loco redneck peckerwood,' Tanner mumbled, but the other men ignored him.

As the three men entered the main street and started towards the livery stable, they felt nervous. They went past several people but no one paid them any attention and they reached the stable without incident.

'So far so good,' Slim said, and went into the stable, his two companions following closely behind.

The balding man who ran the livery stable recognized them immediately and went for a rifle which was propped up against one of the stalls, but Slim crossed to him at speed and stopped him with a powerhouse left hook to the chin. The man's legs buckled beneath him and he fell to the ground, while Slim grabbed the rifle and then stood over the fallen man.

'I oughta kill you,' Slim said. It was obvious from the way the man had reacted, going for his gun like that, that he was part of the rotten deal the sheriff and his cronies had handed out to Slim and his companions. Most likely the livery stable owner would get a cut of the proceeds from selling on their horses.

'I had nothing to do with any of this,' the man said, rubbing his chin. 'Our sheriff is a bad man. All I did is keep your horses safe.'

'What's your name?' Slim asked.

The balding man's face flushed with fear.

'Samuel C. Hayes,' he said. 'Folks just call me Hayes.'

'Good to have a name,' Slim said. 'It comes in mighty handy for a gravestone.'

'I just care for the horses,' Hayes said, a tremor in his voice. He was visibly sweating and his scared eyes darted about, looking at each of the men in turn, pleading for his life.

'Then get up, Hayes,' Slim said, and the man did so.

Tanner went off, located his own horse and patted its head, all the while mumbling soothing words to the beast.

'I just look after the horses,' Hayes said again.

'You got any more guns here?' Slim asked.

For a moment the man didn't answer, but then Slim prodded him in the stomach with the rifle.

'My office,' the man squealed. 'My rig's hanging behind the door and there's a derringer in the top drawer of my desk.'

'Obliged,' Slim said, and motioned for Blackman to go and check.

Blackman did so and then a moment later emerged from the office holding a gunbelt that housed two Navy Colts, while in his free hand he held a single-shot derringer.

Slim smiled.

'This is what's going to happen,' he said, addressing Hayes. 'One of us is gonna stay here with you while we go and have a word with this bad sheriff of yours. While we're gone you're gonna saddle up our horses and get them nice and ready for a quick ride out of here. You make one wrong move and you'll end up with a mighty big hole in your belly.'

The stable owner nodded, hope in

his eyes. Maybe he wasn't going to die after all.

'I don't want no trouble,' he said.

'Then don't make none,' Tanner warned.

With that Slim handed the rifle and derringer to Tanner, telling him to watch the stable owner closely, while he and Blackman armed themselves with a Colt each. Slim wore the gunbelt around his waist and, after checking that both pistols were fully loaded, he and Blackman left the stables.

Once outside they crossed the street, again passing people who were about their daily business, and went directly to the sheriff's office. They couldn't believe how smoothly things were going and, as they pushed through the doors into the office, they found that their luck was holding. The dumb-ass sheriff was sleeping in his chair, his feet up on his desk.

Slim went directly to the lawman and pistol-whipped him across the back of the head, ensuring he wouldn't wake up for a while longer. The sheriff slid from his chair and onto the floor.

'Thief,' Blackman said, and drove a powerful boot into the lawman's stomach. The man groaned but didn't regain consciousness. Slim went through the drawers of the sheriff's desk and found a pair of leg shackles. He tossed them to Blackman.

'Shackle him,' he said. 'And best gag him too.'

'Sure thing,' Blackman said and bent to the lawman. He would take great pleasure from chaining up the sheriff.

'Well, look here,' Slim said, and pulled a large roll of paper money from the bottom drawer. 'This looks like all ours and a good bit more.' He dropped it into his pocket.

'There's our rigs,' Blackman said, as he secured the sheriff's hands behind his back using a length of rope he had found beneath the desk. He pointed to a large glass-fronted cabinet in the corner of the office.

'Good.' Slim went to the cabinet and

removed their gunbelts. He checked them for a moment and then removed three boxes of shells from a shelf. 'Guess we're entitled to a little something extra.' He put on his own gunbelt, immediately feeling better now that he had his own, well-balanced rig, and tossed Blackman's over to him. He threw Tanner's over his shoulder.

Blackman caught his rig and then pulled the star from the sheriff's chest and placed it into his own pocket. 'This may come in handy, you never know.'

The deputy sheriff came through the door.

The man's eyes went first to Slim and Blackman and then to the still unconscious sheriff. He went for his gun and managed to clear leather but not before Slim had a bead on him.

Blackman gasped — he had been riding with Slim for some three months now and he knew the man was fast on the draw, but he had never realized how fast until now. It was as if the gun had instantly appeared there, cocked and aimed, in Slim's hand.

The deputy, realizing he had been bested, dropped his gun and threw his hands up into the air.

'Come here,' Slim said.

The deputy gulped and then cautiously walked over.

'Sorry about this,' Slim said, and pistol-whipped the deputy just as he had the sheriff. The man's legs folded beneath him and he fell to the floor, unconscious.

'Best tie him up with the sheriff and get out of here,' Blackman said.

'Guess so,' Slim said. 'These fellas gonna be mighty sore when they come around. Don't think we should be here then.'

Once the deputy was bound and gagged, Slim and Blackman made their way across the street and back to the livery stable where Tanner waited for them. Again they crossed the street without incident and were soon riding out of town as fast as their horses could carry them, but each of the three men knew that the events of that morning would colour them as outlaws and that things would never be the same again.

4

'We can't just leave Slim tied to a horse,' Tanner said. 'Someone could come along and spot him and then raise the alarm while we're in the bank.'

'Do you think I haven't thought of that?'

'What I don't cotton,' Tanner went on, 'is why we've got to get Slim first? We should rob the bank and if that works out then we get Slim.'

Blackman sighed, feeling as if he'd already explained all this during the ride back to town.

'Because,' he said, 'when we do the bank we need to get away quickly, put as many miles between us and this town as possible before sunup. You never was one for planning and I don't think you should start now.'

'What if we get caught trying to get Slim?' Tanner asked. This plan had more holes than a gold pan. 'We won't be robbing no bank if we're caught getting Slim.'

'We won't get caught,' Blackman said, confidently. 'Slim's in on this with us. He's giving us guidance from beyond.'

Tanner frowned, and then asked, 'And what if there's no money in the bank?'

'Ain't never heard of a bank without money,' Blackman said. 'And besides, whatever we get from the bank, big or small we'll still be leaving town so Slim needs to be ready and waiting for us and not strapped to a wooden frame in the carny tent.'

'Loco redneck peckerwood,' Tanner grumbled.

The two men rode down the main street. They reached their hotel and dismounted, tethering the horses to the hitching post outside. Blackman removed his rifle from its boot and tipped his hat when two men tossed friendly 'howdies' as they walked past.

Tanner nudged Blackman when he

saw the sheriff, a portly-looking man, coming out of the hotel. The lawman's perpetually red face was a picture of ill-health and even in the coolness of the evening he seemed to be sweating. An unkempt beard covered most of the lower half of his face and Blackman could make out traces of gravy amongst the thick whiskers. The sheriff had obviously just enjoyed his evening meal and seemed to be wearing a great deal of it.

'Enjoying the evening, boys?' the sheriff asked.

'Sure thing,' Blackman said and gave the sheriff a wry smile.

'Bit late for an evening ride,' the sheriff said. 'It'll be dark soon.'

Blackman and Tanner exchanged puzzled glances, and the sheriff pointed to their horses.

'We been riding all afternoon,' Tanner said. 'Just got back into town not a few minutes ago.'

The sheriff nodded and looked at the two men for a moment.

There were plenty of men like these drifting around the West; old-timers who had spent their youth chasing dreams that never really panned out, not laying a single root anywhere, and finding themselves, in their twilight years, with nowhere to really call home.

'I guess you old-timers'll be moving on soon,' the sheriff said.

'I kinda like this town,' Tanner said, more for devilment than anything else. He didn't really like the sheriff's tone and had heard similar many times before from lawmen in other towns, other years. Was a time when no one bothered a man and questioned their plans but these days folk were getting too nosy and lawmen more than most were known for sticking their noses in where it weren't wanted.

'We'll be leaving town come first light,' Blackman put in quickly, not wanting to get into a long conversation with the lawman. 'I've got family down South. I figure me and my pard will be welcome to lay our hats there. Time to find somewhere more permanent, I think.'

'We ain't getting any younger,' Tanner said.

'None of us are,' the sheriff nodded, tipped his hat and wandered off, mumbling an extra, 'None of us are,' as he went.

Tanner and Blackman watched as the sheriff made his way down the street and went into his office. They looked across at the carny tent, which was once again doing a brisk trade with Slim's remains. It seemed there was no shortage of customers with a ghoulish streak.

'We'll get our horses all kitted up,' Blackman said. 'Then we'll put them behind the schoolhouse. They won't be seen there so we can hightail it out of here when we're ready.'

'And Slim?'

'We'll tie him to one of our horses. He'll be safe behind the schoolhouse for the time it should take us to get in and out of the bank.'

'I'm gonna get myself something to eat and a drink or two,' Tanner said.

'We'll get a meal in the hotel,' Blackman said. 'But no drink. Not tonight. I need you with a clear head.'

Tanner frowned but it changed to a grudging smile when his old friend slapped an arm around his shoulder and led him into the hotel.

*   *   *

'You stay out here,' Blackman said. 'Keep watch while I untie Slim.'

Tanner nodded, looked up and down the deserted main street and shivered. Winter was on the way and could be felt on the night air. He was getting too old for all this and the cold air was a brutal reminder of that fact.

Blackman removed his knife and cut through the ties that held the door flap to the carny tent closed. It was quicker than untying the rawhide strips and he wanted to get it over with as quickly as possible. Once that was done he nodded to his companion and then vanished into the tent.

It took a moment for his eyes to adjust but he quickly located Slim and then struck a match against his boot heel in order to locate all the straps that held Slim's mummified remains to the frame. In the flickering light of the match Slim's face took on a ghostly pallor and Blackman had to look away as he located and sliced through each of the straps. He had to light a second, and then a third match before the job was done and Slim's body fell free of the wooden frame and into Blackman's waiting arms.

'Ready, Slim,' Blackman said, getting used to the dead man's weight and then dragged him over to the doorway of the tent. 'Everything clear out there?' he whispered through the doorway.

'Yeah,' Tanner replied.

'Then here comes Slim.' Blackman started to push his old friend's body through the doorway. 'Grab hold of him.'

For one split second Blackman felt a

shock as Slim's body was pulled forward. It was as if his old pard had returned to life as he disappeared through the tent flap.

Blackman went through immediately afterwards.

'Let's get him to the horses,' Blackman said and grabbed Slim by one arm while Tanner held the other. As they crossed the street they looked like two men leading a drunken, and rather stiff, man home.

'He's as stiff as a board,' Tanner said, as they reached the old schoolhouse and started up the banking that led to the rear of the building.

'He would be.' Blackman sounded annoyed. 'He's dead.'

'Then how we gonna put him over a horse?' Tanner asked, and gasped as they neared the top of the bank. Slim may have not had any real weight to him but the banking was toil enough all on its own. 'For us to put him over a horse depends on him being pliable. He's rigid.'

'We'll sit him upright,' Blackman said. 'Tie him that way.'

'Well, you're riding with him,' Tanner said. 'I ain't.'

'Slim's our friend and he needs our help,' Blackman said.

'He's dead,' Tanner retorted.

'True friendship continues long after living is gone,' Blackman replied and grunted as he tried to manhandle the remains of his old friend. 'So shut up and help me get him to the horses.'

'Loco redneck peckerwood,' Tanner grumbled.

If the three of them had been seen as they went around the rear of the schoolhouse, it is debatable just what any witnesses would have assumed they had just seen. They could have taken it as three men looking for somewhere to bed down for the night, or then again they could have been taken for two men and a wax dummy, or even something more outlandish, for the possibilities were endless. It was however unlikely that anyone would have realized that what they were actually seeing was two ageing outlaws and the corpse of an infamous bad man of the West.

'Get him in the saddle,' Blackman said, and he cupped his hands beneath one of Slim's feet and lifted him up towards the horse. Tanner stretched to guide Slim, as Blackman tossed the dead man's legs up and over. Eventually they had Slim seated in the saddle, though leaning would have been more descriptive as he fell forward, his legs reaching out rigidly towards the rear of the horse.

Slim took a rope from his saddlebags and threw it over Slim and the horse, tying it tightly around the saddle horn.

'That should do it,' he said, and stood back, looking at Slim seated upon the horse.

5

'Now for the moment of truth,' Blackman said, as he pushed the key into the lock. It was a perfect fit and he smiled as he turned it and heard the heavy lock release itself. He pushed on the bank door and it opened slightly.

'Well I'll be a woodchuck from Wisconsin,' Tanner said, 'Maybe old Slim really does have a hand in this from the hereafter.'

'Make no mistake,' Blackman whispered. 'Slim's with us tonight.'

The thought sent a shiver down Tanner's spine and he smiled weakly. Ordinarily he would have scoffed at the suggestion and likely hurled one of his usual insults at his pard, but here during the dead of night it seemed quite plausible that ghosts could walk the world.

Blackman looked up and down the

street, and once satisfied that all was clear he pushed the door open wider.

He turned to his companion.

'Best you stay out here on lookout,' he said. 'Keep out of sight and whistle if you see anyone. We don't want this to go wrong when we're so close.'

Tanner nodded.

'Suits me fine,' he said. 'Be as quick as you can.'

Blackman wriggled his fingers. 'Been a while,' he said, 'but I reckon I still got the touch.'

'Just get it done.'

Blackman nodded and went inside, closing the door behind him.

The silence of the bank seemed absolute to Blackman as he closed the door. For several moments he stood perfectly still, allowing his eyes to adjust to the darkness. He didn't want to light a match until it was absolutely necessary to do so. The town was asleep at this ungodly hour but there was always a chance someone would be wandering the streets and notice the flickering flames dancing across the windows. He carried the stub of a candle in one of his pockets and figured on only using it when he worked on the safe itself.

Best be extra careful.

Blackman peered around the room and saw a doorway behind the long oak counter that led to an anteroom.

Not wanting to trip over anything, he cautiously made his way to the counter and felt along its edge for an opening. He found one and lifted the hinged lid and made his way behind it. Once there he did risk lighting a match, but even then he knelt before lighting it so as to keep the light at ground level. Using the flickering flame he checked for obstacles, but there were none that he could see, other than a couple of wooden chairs which he could negotiate his way around, and so he made his way to the anteroom.

There was a thick curtain hanging from the opening to the anteroom and Blackman went inside and closed it behind him. Now, he figured, it would be safe to use the candle and so he fished in his pocket to locate it and once he had done so he took a match to the wick. It took a moment for the candle to catch but as soon as it did it sent out an orange tinged glow, which illuminated all but the shadowy corners of the room.

Blackman crept forward and frowned when he failed to locate a bank safe of any kind. It had to be somewhere in this small room, though where it could be hidden he had no idea. He looked around himself, seeing no obvious place for the safe to be stored.

'Come on, Slim,' he mumbled. 'Where the hell is the safe?'

This wasn't good and didn't make any sense. This was a bank. There had to be a safe. All this room seemed to be used for was storage and there were stacks of paperwork, all neatly tied and labelled, on almost every surface in the room.

There was another door at the far end of the anteroom and Blackman went to it, opened it and peered into an even smaller room than the one he now stood in. It wasn't so much a room as a closet.

Almost immediately a huge smile crossed his face, for there in the room was a large chest safe. He quickly went inside and held the candle up to the door of the safe and his smile grew even wider, for there, moulded in the cast iron doors, was the trademark — Parker Safe Co.

He'd opened many a Parker in his day.

$\star$ $\star$ $\star$

Tanner heard the approach of the lone rider long before he saw him, and he immediately fell to the ground and hid himself behind the picket fence. He crawled across to the bank door and pushed it open slightly.

'Blackman,' he whispered, but received no answer and so he called louder. There was still no answer and so he placed fingers in his mouth, each side of his curled tongue and gave a whistle.

'What?' Blackman called back.

'I think someone's coming.'

'Who?'

'I don't know.' Tanner shook his head, thinking that his pard was being particularly stupid. 'I heard someone riding into town.'

'I'm nearly done,' Blackman said. 'I've only got a couple of tumblers to go. In a few minutes I'll have this thing open.'

'Someone's coming,' Tanner repeated.

'Just keep out of sight, keep quiet. Likely whoever it is will ride straight past.'

'Loco,' Tanner grumbled, and crawled back over to the picket fence where he'd be able to see the rider, whoever it was, as they entered town. Now he slid his iron from its leather and held it in his hand, his finger teasing the trigger. He had no intention of shooting unless he positively had to, but all the same the gun gave him a little comfort.

The sound of the horse clopping

down the street was louder now and, as Tanner looked between the slats of the fence he could make out the shadowy figure of a rider at the far end of the main street. The rider, little more than a shadow at the moment, seemed to be sitting awkwardly in the saddle as if hurt.

Damn, Tanner thought.

That was all they needed at the moment.

Someone coming into town with some kind of injury and waking the sawbones.

It would be even worse if outlaws or Indians had injured the anonymous rider.

If that was the case then the sheriff would also be roused and maybe even a posse thrown together. With all that activity there would be no way he and Blackman would be able to slip out of town with their long-dead pard.

'Damn,' Tanner spat into the ground and allowed one of his hands to rest over the butt of his Colt. Shooting was the last thing he wanted but it often paid to be prepared and so he lay there, hardly daring to breathe as the rider continued on down the main street.

★ ★ ★

Yesteryear

'RUTHLESS GUNMEN KILL DEPUTY IN COLD BLOOD AND ARE VALIANTLY FOUGHT OFF BY SHERIFF DEKE DAWKINS,' Slim read the newspaper article out loud for the benefit of his companions. He slapped the newspaper against a knee, not believing the lies he was reading. 'That ain't how it happened.'

Blackman smiled, wryly.

'It's in the newspaper,' he said. 'Folk will believe it.'

Slim nodded, knowing that this was indeed the case.

'Read the rest of it,' Tanner said, eagerly. 'Is my name mentioned?'

'No,' Slim said, as he quickly skimmed through the article. 'Mine is, though.'

Tanner seemed disappointed. 'Don't I even get a mention?' he asked.

'Slim McCord,' Slim quoted directly from the article, 'and his two blood-thirsty companions.'

'That's us,' Tanner smiled. 'His two blood-thirsty companions.'

'Read the rest of it,' Blackman said, and shook his head in Tanner's direction. Anyone would think that he wanted to be dubbed a vicious outlaw killer.

Slim smoothed the newspaper out some and then read the entire article from the top.

The gist of the story was that the three of them, that's Slim McCord and his 'two blood-thirsty companions', had gone into the sheriff's office and, without warning, opened fire, killing the young deputy who left a widow and three young children. It was only the bravery of the town sheriff, one Deke Dawkins, formerly of Colorado, that saved his own life. He'd struggled with the three outlaws but was overpowered by superior numbers and pistol-whipped to the floor. The three outlaws, who had previously been run out of town as undesirables, proceeded to plunder the office, which contained the entire town funds, which had been raised for the erection of a new courthouse. This totalled some $6,000, which the sheriff had earlier that day removed from the town bank so that it could be paid to the relevant and correct parties. This, the newspaper concluded, was a major setback for Hope Springs as work was due to begin on the construction of the courthouse the coming week.

'Damn lies,' Slim said. 'It's all damn lies.'

'How much did we get from that sheriff?' Blackman asked.

'A little over two thousand dollars,' Slim said.

Blackman whistled. 'And the sheriff claims six,' he said.

'Worse,' Slim said. 'He also pegs us as killers.'

'We didn't kill anyone,' Tanner

grumbled. 'We left that deputy alive and we didn't steal no six grand either.'

Slim crumpled the newspaper and threw it into the dirt. He had been standing, leaning against a tree, and now he sat himself down, his back to the tree, his legs stretched out before him.

'Newspaper's nothing but lies,' said Blackman, who had retrieved the newspaper and smoothed it out. He wasn't that much of a reader but he could make out most of the article.

They had been hiding out in the hills above the town of Cassidy for a few days now, resting their horses as well as themselves before moving on. They had figured they'd ride west towards cattle country and see if they could hire themselves on as hands with one herd or another, maybe raise some money and then hit some booming frontier town and remain there for the coming winter. That had been the plan and earlier Slim had taken a ride on into Cassidy in order to purchase provisions for the trip ahead. They had all been in good spirits about moving on, the events that had befallen them in Hope Springs were all but forgotten, but that had quickly changed when Slim had returned with the newspaper in his hands.

'We're known as killers now,' Slim said. 'Bloodthirsty killers. Likely there'll be enough of a bounty on our heads to attract the worst of the bounty hunters. Everywhere we go we'll have to keep a look over our shoulders for those killers.'

'And the law,' Tanner said. 'Don't forget the law.'

'That sheriff,' Blackman complained, 'I did not shoot the deputy.'

'Sheriff must have killed the deputy himself,' Slim said, trying to work out a likely chain of events.

'Don't make no sense,' said Tanner, never the brightest button in a box. 'Why would the sheriff want to gun down his own deputy?'

'Likely the sheriff played us,' Slim

said. 'Likely he'd figured we would return to town if he robbed us of all our money and possessions. Likely he was banking on us returning.'

'That don't make no sense,' Blackman said. 'What are you saying?'

And so Slim explained his theory as best he could.

Slim doubted if there had been any town funds in the sheriff's office and figured it most likely that the fat lawman had swindled the money away long before that. Maybe someone in the bank was involved in the fraud with the sheriff — had to be really, since the newspaper had said that the money had recently been withdrawn from the town bank. Slim guessed that the fraud was about to come to light, that maybe folks were due to get paid. The sheriff and his fellow fraudsters would have been running around like headless chickens trying to figure out what they could do, how they could explain the missing money, and so when the three drifting cowboys rode into town it would have seemed like the answer to their dreams.

That was the way Slim had figured it — it certainly explained how they had found it so easy to simply ride back into town and overpower the sheriff, although the lawman couldn't have known he'd be pistol-whipped. It could have been the lawman's plan to allow them to get the drop on him. It was a risky hand to play but Slim guessed a seasoned poker player like the sheriff would have been willing to bet they wouldn't kill him, that they weren't that kind of men. That's likely why the $2,000 had been so easy to find. Would the sheriff really keep such a large sum in his desk drawer? According to the newspaper he had kept a lot more than that there.

It all made perfect sense.

The sheriff must have shot the deputy himself, figuring no doubt, that when the three men were caught with $2,000 of the money on them, then they would either be shot and killed or strung up like Christmas turkeys. The posse, likely every able-bodied man from the town, wouldn't believe a word the three drifters said and would be angry enough to forgo a fair trial and dispense frontier justice there and then.

'Son of a bitch!' Blackman said.

'We should have killed him,' Tanner snapped, angrily.

'Well, we certainly wouldn't have been in any more trouble if we had,' Slim said.

'I'd be a heck of a lot more satisfied.' Blackman spat into the ground. He took the makings from his pocket and quickly constructed a quirly, which he placed between his teeth. He struck a match on the underside of a boot and greedily sucked in the smoke.

Silence fell between the three men as each of them mulled over the full implications of the newspaper's story. In the distance a hawk gave out a cry as it sailed on the gentle morning breeze and above them thick clouds began to form in a sky that only moments ago had been nothing but the big blue.

'Guess there ain't much we can do

about it all,' Blackman said, finally.

'I sure hope we meet up with that sheriff again someday.' Tanner spat in the dirt and then pulled up his collar against the sudden chill.

'We will,' Slim said, getting back to his feet and dusting himself down. 'I'm going to put this right.'

Blackman and Tanner exchanged puzzled glances and then looked at the man, who had become their leader. They had been together but a short time but the natural dynamic of their relationship had already been formed. They were friends more than anything else, and certainly didn't think of themselves as a gang no matter what the newspaper article had said, but the force of Slim's personality had made him their natural leader.

'We're going back to Hope Springs,' Slim said. 'Clear our names.'

'You loco?' Tanner asked, and then broke eye contact when Slim gave him a steely look. He nervously scraped at the dirt beneath him with his fingers.

'We ride into Hope Springs and we'll be arrested,' Blackman said, shaking his head. 'You think we just tell them we didn't shoot no deputy and only took two thousand dollars, a good deal of which was rightly ours, and that that will be the end of it?'

'I don't care about clearing our name with anyone but one person,' Slim said. 'I'd sure like to kill that sheriff, though.'

'I think we'd all like to kill that sheriff,' Blackman said. 'But no one would believe anything we said and chances are we'd be gunned down before we had much chance to speak. The sheriff would make sure of that.'

'I guess so,' Slim said and went to his horse and pulled out a slice of jerky from his saddle-bags. He bit off a chunk and thoughtfully chewed on it.

'Then I say we put a few more miles between us and Hope Springs,' Blackman said and Tanner nodded and mumbled in agreement.

'We've got two thousand dollars,' Slim said. 'You boys can keep your share but I plan on tracking down that deputy's widow and giving her mine. I'll make sure she believes me; tell her to pass on my story to the territorial marshal's office or the army maybe. Someone needs to look into that sheriff's affairs.'

'You ain't wrong there,' Blackman said.

'The man from the livery stable was in on the rotten deal,' Slim said. 'He'd likely know what the sheriff had done. Likely he went straight around and untied the sheriff when we left town. The way the newspaper told it the sheriff wasn't overpowered and shackled, the deputy neither, so someone must have released them. I'm guessing it was that man Hayes.'

Blackman nodded: that made perfect sense.

'Guess I may call on him first,' Slim said. 'The way I see it Hayes must have been there when the sheriff gunned down the deputy. I don't know why but it's likely the deputy had to be silenced, that he wasn't in on the rotten dealing with his boss.'

'What do we do?' Blackman stood directly in front of Slim, eyes locked, as if they were gunfighters sizing each other up. 'Find that widow and just waltz in there and say sorry we killed your husband but here's some cash money! No hard feelings!'

'We didn't kill her husband,' Slim said. His tone was cold, matter of fact.

Blackman looked at Slim for a moment. 'You're serious about this?' he said.

'Deadly,' Slim nodded.

'You really are loco,' Blackman said, and then exchanged a glance with Tanner. 'We ain't got much of a stake as it is. If we gotta live like outlaws then that two grand will be needed to see us through the winter.'

'The widow's needs are greater than ours.' Slim took his makings from his pocket and put together a smoke. 'If we're gonna be named outlaws then we may as well become outlaws. We can get more money — we could pull a robbery somewhere down the trail, even find some work, or win a card game maybe. That widow's gonna find winter a struggle with young children to raise, and when those children cry themselves to sleep at night it will be my name they'll think of when they remember their father.'

'And us two blood-thirsty companions,' Tanner said.

'Sure,' Blackman said. 'But the blood's on the sheriff's hands not ours.'

'I'm going back,' Slim insisted, and both of his companions knew him well enough to realize that further argument was as useless as a two dollar whore at a temperance meeting.

Blackman stared open-mouthed at Slim for a moment, before laughing and then shaking his head.

'Then I guess I'm with you,' he said.

Tanner, still sitting on the ground, looked at the two men, thinking that they were both loco. He got to his feet and whipped his hat against his pants to dust himself off.

'I say we just give the widow a thousand,' he said. 'Keep some for ourselves.'

'We'll keep a hundred apiece,' Slim said, with a tight smile. Not for a moment had he doubted the loyalty of his friends.

'A hundred apiece it is,' Tanner said, and walked over to his horse, all the while muttering beneath his breath.

'Then saddle up,' Slim said. 'Hope Springs it is.'

'Looks like a storm's heading our way,' Blackman said, as he pulled himself up into his saddle. He patted the side of his horse's head and then took a handful of oats from his saddle-bags and palmed them into the horse's mouth.

'There's sure enough a storm coming to Hope Springs,' Slim said and climbed up into his own saddle. He spurred the horse into movement and took up the lead as they started in the direction they had come from.

'Loco,' Tanner said and spurred his own horse off in pursuit of his two friends.

6

The rider was getting closer, seemingly in no rush, leaning forward in the saddle while the horse made its way down the main street. Tanner felt his heart miss a beat as he realized just who the rider was.

'Slim?' he said.

How was this possible?

It wasn't possible!

Possible or not this was Blackman's horse coming towards him with Slim in the saddle. There was no mistaking that fact.

The rider wasn't so much leaning forward as lying rigid, legs outstretched towards the rear of the horse. And there was no mistaking that horse either with that flame shaped splatter of white on its forehead.

Yep, it was Slim — good old, dead old Slim had decided to take a leisurely ride down the main street. The way he was silhouetted by the moonlight which was high above his slumped head, looked incredibly ghostly and for a brief moment Tanner felt his blood run cold as a sweat broke out on his brow. He immediately felt foolish and told himself there was no such thing as ghosts and that folk, not even Slim, didn't return from the dead.

'Gone is gone,' he mumbled, giving his thoughts voice.

Tanner stepped out of concealment and made his way into the centre of the street, watching as Slim approached. He felt a shiver run the length of his spine and he half expected his late friend to suddenly reanimate and start yelling loud enough to wake the dead; his fellow dead.

'Damn!' Tanner cursed, as the horse and rider came level with him and he realized, with a sigh of relief, just what had happened.

Slim hadn't suddenly sprung back to life and decided to come to their aid.

He was still as dead as dead could be and it looked as if the reins of the horse had worked loose and that the dumb beast had come in search of its master. It was just the sort of thing a peckerwood's horse was apt to do.

Tanner raised his hands, stopping the horse and then grabbed its reins and started to lead it back up the street to the schoolhouse. He walked slowly, not wanting to disturb anyone in the still sleeping town.

Slim, of course, said nothing.

*　*　*

Blackman couldn't believe his eyes.

He'd opened the Parker easily enough, feeling great pride in his old skill as he heard the last of those tumblers pop and the lock disengage itself. He still had it, could still work that old magic, and he'd wriggled the fingers on each hand in a celebratory boast as he opened the cast-iron door and peered at the contents inside.

'Sweet Mother of Mercy!' Blackman said and counted the money for the second time, feeling that he'd made a mistake initially. There couldn't have been that much in there, not in a small town bank like this.

He came up with the same figure.

There had been no mistake. $59,000.

$59,000, mostly made up of hundreds but with some twenties, the odd bundle of tens and a few singles.

The safe had also contained a stack of deeds, as well as a pile of official-looking paperwork but Blackman left all that alone.

Blackman had brought a large flour sack with him, which he pulled from his shirt where it had nestled, folded against his stomach, and he quickly transferred the money into it. Once the bag was full and tied he took another look around and noticed three one-dollar bills on the floor. They must have dropped from the pile as he'd stuffed the money into the sack. He scooped them up and placed them into his shirt pocket.

$59,000.

An incredible haul, an *unbelievable* haul, and once again Blackman felt as if Slim had a hand in all this, that he had been protecting them from the Hereafter. He looked towards the ceiling but saw the heavens as he mouthed a silent, 'thank you'.

Time to go.

Blackman groaned as he got to his feet. Damn these old bones, he thought, but immediately felt better when he realized that he and his old bones would spend the rest of his life in luxury.

He blew out the candle, placed it in the safe and then closed the heavy door; spinning the dial and hearing the tumblers slide into the locked configuration. Then he kissed the tip of the fingers on his right hand and affectionately touched the safe door before carefully making his way back to the front of the bank. Once there he opened the front door slowly and slipped out into the moonlight.

He looked for Tanner, couldn't see him, but without dwelling on it, he placed the sack on the ground and, once more using the key he'd found, locked the door. Once that was done he pushed the key back through the letterbox and smiled when he heard it hit the floor inside.

Then he picked the sack up again and once more looked for Tanner.

There was no sign of his friend and, sack slung over one shoulder, free hand filled with iron, Blackman made his way to the street. He immediately saw Tanner coming down the street towards him.

'You were supposed to keep watch,' Blackman said as Tanner reached him.

Tanner was short on breath and he panted as he spoke.

'I had to,' he said and took several deep breaths. 'I had to, had to . . . never mind I'll tell you later. How much?' His eyes pointed to the sack over Blackman's shoulder.

Blackman smiled.

7

Possum Creek was a little over thirty years old. It had started out as an army outpost before becoming a trail town; the main street compacted harder than stone by the herds the cowboys would drive through town. In those early days the town had grown quickly, getting fat on the money the herds brought in. A few hundred thirsty and lusty cowboys tended to generate a lot of income and most weeks the town saw one outfit or another arriving to stop off and enjoy the facilities before moving on with their arduous cattle drives. The first building of note was a hotel, which was quickly followed by a saloon, gambling house and livery stable. Settlers came in, attracted by the booming nature of the cow town, and started building their own homes, forming a community amongst the madness of the largely transient population.

Eventually the residents outnumbered the transients and by that time the town had acquired a schoolhouse, civic building, two more saloons, a jailhouse and sheriff's office, as well as a barber, doctor and dentist. Possum Creek was no longer a lonely little outpost but a real town, a permanent part of the landscape. It had survived the war and, thanks to the railroads, prospered afterwards, and even if things had tailed off in recent years, the cattle no longer coming into town, it remained a vibrant community. The nature of the town had changed many times over the years, but it still retained a little of that cow town rowdiness in its foundations.

It was certainly rowdy this morning, rowdier than most folks, who hadn't been here during the early years, could remember.

It was a little after nine when Theo Fowler, the manager of the town bank, burst into the sheriff's office with the news that during the night someone had robbed the bank. He didn't have any idea how it had happened. There was no sign of a forced entry, but when the safe had been opened for business that morning, all it had contained was a burnt out candle and a stack of paperwork. There had been over $50,000, the bulk of the bank's business these past two months not to mention a large sum of Government money intended for tribal payouts, in the safe.

The bank manager had decided not to mention that he had previously lost the key to the bank, the key which had turned up on the bank floor this morning, and obviously been used by the intruders to gain entry. That wasn't something the bank manager felt should be made public knowledge. He hoped he'd be able to keep it a strictly private embarrassment.

Sheriff Bud Caxton wasn't at all happy with the news. He liked to keep a quiet town and bank robberies were certainly not conducive to a peaceful life. Even bank robberies where the robbers appeared to have spirited themselves into the bank and then spirited themselves away just as quickly. And if that wasn't enough to give the sour-faced sheriff a gut ache, that damn carny man, Tom Ryder, had come into the office a little later, screaming that his star exhibit had been stolen sometime during the night. The barker was livid with anger and he yelled at the sheriff, demanding something be done.

Was there a connection between the two events? The sheriff felt that there must have been but for the life of him he couldn't make out just what that connection was. Body snatching and bank robbery was a combination the sheriff didn't think he'd ever heard of before.

And now as Caxton crossed the street and went into his office, he was aware of the speculation going on around town. The news that the bank had been robbed had spread like wildfire among the residents and the fact that someone had also taken the remains of infamous outlaw Slim McCord only added colour to the story.

There were those, the sheriff had heard, who claimed that the outlaw had returned from the dead and carried out the bank robbery himself. That was hogwash of course, but some folk gave it credence simply because there was no sign of any break-in at the bank. They claimed that the dead man had simply walked through the bank walls and then spirited the money away. What a dead man, someone seemingly removed from material needs, could want with a stack of money was anyone's guess. During his life Slim McCord had been blamed for more than one bank robbery, and now in death he was having yet another attributed to his name.

'This will ruin the bank,' Fowler said, coming into the office behind the sheriff and closing the door behind him.

'Won't do much for the people who had money in the bank, neither,' the sheriff said and stared at the bank manager. The man was proving to be a massive pain in the arse with his constant whining.

'We're insured,' Fowler said. 'All our investors from businesses to the single man are protected. They'll get their money, but the bank will never recover. Unless we get that money back we're finished.'

'We'll sure try and get the money back,' the sheriff said, fearing that this wouldn't be the case. The robbers, whoever they were, had too much of a start on them and, besides, the sheriff wasn't at all sure of what had actually happened here. If Fowler was to be believed, someone had gotten into the bank leaving no visible signs, and then opened the safe, not blown it open, mind, but opened it with the combination. This was all strange enough but even stranger still was the theft of that mummified outlaw from the carny.

'Try!' Fowler almost choked on the

words. 'I should hope you'd do more than just try.'

'Look.' The sheriff eased his bulk into his chair and took a cigar from the box on his desk. He sucked the smoke to life and then spoke through a cloud of dense smoke. 'You say someone broke into the bank and yet there's no sign of any forced entry and then, you say, they opened the safe with the combination.'

The fury in Fowler's face was replaced by anxiety. He crossed the room and sank into the only other chair in the office.

'There are men,' he said, 'not many but some, who can break even the most complicated of safes. Granted these men are rare but I've seen demonstrations. These men have some kind of enhanced ability, it comes naturally to them and they can feel those tumblers moving within the safe. There are men who can do this.'

'Maybe,' the sheriff said, though it sounded like something out of a bad dime novel to him. 'But how did this rare man get into the bank in the first place?'

The bank manager blushed, leant forward on his knees, and then buried his face in his hands.

'Can I have the utmost secrecy?' he asked.

The sheriff frowned. 'Don't get your meaning,' he said.

'What I'm about to tell you must not become public knowledge,' Fowler said. 'It will be the ruin of me.'

The sheriff nodded. 'Go on,' he prompted.

And so Fowler told him of the key to the bank. Of how he had discovered it was missing, and felt that he had left it somewhere at home, despite usually being so fastidious with it. He wasn't sure what had happened to the damn key. Maybe it had somehow been stolen from him. He just didn't have any idea. One moment the key was missing and then the next it turned up on the floor the morning following the robbery. The robber, or robbers, had posted it back through the letterbox.

'What I should have done,' Fowler concluded, 'is get the locks to the bank changed, but that would have taken a couple of days, and been a major inconvenience. I was so sure the key would turn up.'

'It did turn up,' the sheriff said, and although he was no great shakes at his own job he felt that this bank manager was totally incompetent.

Fowler nodded and produced the offending key from his pocket.

'We've got to find these men,' he said, and sank further into despair.

'We will,' the sheriff said, feeling some sympathy for the other man. 'My deputy's out now raising a posse. They'll find them.'

'I hope so,' Fowler said. 'I do hope so.'

At that moment the door flew open and once again the flamboyant figure of the carny barker filled the doorway.

'What's being done to find my

mummy?' he asked.

'He wants his mummy,' the sheriff joked, but the humour was lost on Fowler who seemed to be sitting on a precipice of doom.

Ryder came into the office and slammed the door behind him. He looked at Fowler with obvious distaste and then glared at the sheriff.

'That mummy,' he said, 'is very valuable to me. I demand the law does something to find it.'

The sheriff stood to his full height and clenched his fists until the knuckles glowed a bony white.

'We'll find your mummy,' he said, oblivious to how ridiculous the words sounded, spoken as they were to a middle-aged loud-mouth carny barker. 'My deputy is putting together a posse and they'll be riding out shortly. We've had a bank robbery and we figure that whoever robbed the bank also took your mummy. Why that is, I ain't got the foggiest, but we'll get them.'

Ryder looked as if he was about to

yell back at the sheriff but then he thought better of it. He tossed another contemptuous look at Fowler and then shook his head.

'I want my mummy,' he repeated, and retreated from the sheriff's office.

8

Maybe Slim was with them after all, Tanner thought, as he pondered on the latest unlikely event to have befallen them.

They had ridden out of Possum Creek significantly richer than they had been entering the town, and after maybe riding an hour into the hills, they had come across a fully saddled horse just standing there, feeding on the long grasses. There had been no sign of the horse's owner and so the two men had untied Slim and placed him on the horse.

It was as if the horse had been waiting there for them, as if Slim had used some supernatural influence to place it there, spirited it into existence where they were sure to come across it. The horse, pale in colour, was just the sort of beast Tanner imagined a ghost would ride through the trails of the hereafter.

It was just another strange occurrence in a string of strange occurrences.

As Blackman had pointed out they had only ridden into Possum Creek on a whim, and almost immediately come across the carny, which had the body of their old friend as an exhibit. The chances of that happening in a well-ordered world seemed remote, and yet happened it had. Then the bank manager had lost the key to the bank, dropped it right in Blackman's sight, and there turns out to be so much money in the safe, which Blackman had managed to open so easily despite not having cracked a safe in more than a decade. Now, finding it slow going having to ride with Slim's body tied to one of their horses, they had come across another in the middle of nowhere.

Life was taking one strange turn after another.

They rode in silence, the third horse

carrying Slim, tied to a rope that was wrapped around the pommel of Blackman's saddle, trailing along behind them. Tanner kept glancing back at Slim, half expecting the dead man to suddenly start talking to them.

At this point nothing would have surprised him.

'You know,' Blackman said and took a glance over his shoulder at Slim, 'we'll ride maybe another day, put more distance between us and Possum Creek and then find somewhere suitable to bury old Slim.'

Tanner nodded.

'Somewhere where the grave'll get the sun,' he said. 'Slim always did like the sun.'

'You reckon he's looking down on us now?' Blackman asked. 'Sure feels that way.'

Tanner looked back at Slim and then cast his eyes to the sky above them.

'I hope so,' he said. 'I sure do hope so.'

Blackman looked up at the sky,

checking the sun's position and wondered if a posse had left Possum Creek yet. He figured they must have by now as he guessed it was somewhere around noon. They had a good head start and had ridden through the night, covering a good many miles before dawn had broken. By the time the robbery had been discovered back in Possum Creek, Blackman figured they had already put a goodly distance between them and the town.

'We'll keep riding till sundown,' Blackman said. 'Only take short breaks to water the horses. I reckon it will be safe to set up camp somewhere tonight.'

'We're gonna need to,' Tanner nodded. They were travelling at an easy pace but all the same it was tiring. He had been in the saddle for hours now and the old man was starting to feel his age in a way that he had never done before. 'I'm tuckered out.'

Blackman laughed and then patted the sack which he'd tied to his saddle.

'Think of all the comfort you'll be

able to buy with this,' he said. 'Our last job, pulled off by the three of us, Slim included, and we're rich. We're rich!' He whooped out in delight, so loud that he startled his horse to such a point that he had to dig in his spurs to bring the beast back under control. Slim was thrown about on the horse behind but the ties held, and the mummified outlaw didn't seem at all bothered by the sudden commotion.

'Loco redneck peckerwood,' Tanner muttered.

* * *

The posse was ten miles out of town when they came across the man. Dressed like a city dude, and carrying a battered carpetbag, the man was dishevelled, exhausted and close to unconsciousness when they had discovered him.

'Snake spooked my horse,' the man said. 'I was thrown and the dumb horse ran off into the wilderness. Couldn't find the dumb beast anywhere. I've walked miles.'

'Ain't nothing dumb about running from a rattler,' Deputy Rawlings said.

The man looked up at the deputy, said nothing, and smiled weakly.

There were sniggers from most of the men in the posse. They were silenced when Deputy Sam Rawlings raised a gloved hand.

'Don't see nothing to laugh at,' he said. 'Someone get this man some water.'

Pete Glover reached down and pulled his canteen from his saddle-bags. He tossed it to the ground.

The man bent, picked it up and, after struggling with the screw cap, drank greedily. The man was slightly built and it seemed his spindly legs would collapse beneath him at any moment, but he remained upright while he drank his fill.

'Thank you,' he said.

'Where you heading?' the deputy shifted in his saddle.

'Possum Creek,' the man said. 'Though anywhere where I can get a room for a night or two and buy another horse would be a start.' The man frowned and then reached into his carpetbag and pulled out a business card, which he handed to the deputy.

The deputy read the card: G.M. Dobbs. Man of Letters.

'Dobbs.' The deputy looked at the man for a moment. 'What's your business Mr Dobbs?'

'I'm a writer,' the man said.

'A writer?'

The man looked at the deputy and then nodded.

'Yes, sir,' he said. 'I am.'

'What do you write?'

'Newspaper articles, mostly,' the man said. 'But I've done the odd dime novel, adventure stories, potboilers, that kind of thing. Maybe you men have read some of my work.'

If any of the posse had indeed read anything written by the spindly-looking man none of them was going to admit it and they remained silent.

'I was heading for the town of Possum Creek to take up a position with the *Chronicle* newspaper,' the writer continued. 'That's why I was riding around this wilderness when my darn fool horse bolted.'

Again there were sniggers from the posse and once again the deputy silenced his men with a firm hand.

'The *Chronicle*'s run by J.B. Wilson,' the deputy said. 'He's a good man and Possum Creek's but maybe ten miles that way.' He pointed in the direction he had come.

The man nodded. He looked at each of the riders in turn and then turned back to the deputy.

'Don't suppose you'd have a spare horse?' he asked. 'I don't think I could walk another step. Not with my feet. I've always been a martyr to my poor old feet.'

'Well we don't have a remuda,' the deputy said. 'Didn't figure we'd need one.'

The man shrugged his shoulders and walked across and handed the canteen back to the man who had tossed it.

'Thank you, kindly,' he said, and the cowboy nodded.

The deputy turned in his saddle and then addressed a short balding man called Carver. 'Let this writer fella double up with you. Take him into town, introduce him to Wilson.'

'But,' Carver said, clearly not relishing the task of taking the spindly-looking man into town, 'the posse'll be a man down. I'm not likely to catch up with you.'

'No matter,' the deputy said. 'We can't leave this fella out here alone. A pen won't be much defence if the coyotes take a liking to him.'

'Thank you,' the man said. 'Thank you so very much.'

Carver shook his head and guided his horse over to the man. He reached down a hand, telling the writer to climb up. The man did so but almost fell back down and Carver had to grab him by the back of the pants and pull him into the saddle.

'If you can do without me why bring me along in the first place?' Carver grumbled, clearly not pleased that he had been chosen to baby-sit this greenhorn writer. What the hell good was a writer out here? He spurred his horse off back towards town. The man seated behind him gripped him tightly around the waist, as if afraid he would fall back off.

The deputy watched Carver vanish down the trail, the writer holding on to him and being tossed about in the saddle. With Carver gone the posse was now down to six men, including the deputy, but that didn't matter none. The deputy felt he had enough men to handle whatever turned out to be ahead of them.

'Let's go catch some bad men,' the deputy said, and spurred his horse forward.

★ ★ ★

They had ridden directly into town, coming from the east so as to avoid any posse out looking for them, and although the main street was bustling they didn't get any special attention as they mingled in with the other traffic. Slim took up the lead, once again going directly towards the livery stable. For a moment Slim was about to dismount, but then he shrugged his shoulders, spurring his horse forward and straight into the stable.

Hayes, who had been sweeping out one of the stalls, looked up and his face lost all colour as he recognized Slim. He dropped the sweeping brush and tried to get out of the stall but Slim sent his horse forward, blocking off the man's exit.

Blackman and Tanner suddenly came in, both of them, like Slim, still on horseback. Each of the three men quickly dismounted and Tanner took up position beside the entrance so he could watch the street, while Blackman, gun in hand, went over to Slim.

Slim pushed his horse back from the door to the stall and then stood there, his Colt aimed directly between Hayes's eyes.

'Come out of there,' he said.

'I just look after the horses,' Hayes said, going through the same spiel he'd used the last time they were here. 'I just want an easy life. Look after my stables and be left alone. That's all I want.'

'Shut up,' Slim said, coldly. He was in no mood to play around with this whining fool, not when some deputy lay cold and dead. The time for fooling had long gone and Slim knew that this whining runt of a man was in this mess right up to his scrawny neck. 'Now get out of there. I want to talk to you.'

The man came from the stall, hands held up above his head and Slim forcefully pushed him backwards, off his feet. The man landed with a squeal and then sat up, arms resting on his knees. He looked at Slim and Blackman, his eyes once more pleading, but this time something told the livery stable owner that he wasn't going to get any mercy from these men, and that the only way he might live was by doing whatever they said.

'Talk,' he nodded. 'Sure, I can talk. Talking is a nice friendly way to pass the time. I can sure do that.'

'Good,' Slim said and knelt so he was level with the small man. He kept his gun aimed directly at him. 'Now tell me what happened?'

'I don't follow.'

'The newspapers say we killed a deputy,' Slim said. 'Took a lot of money.'

The man nodded. 'Yeah, I heard,' he said.

'We didn't though,' Slim said. 'So who did?'

'I just look after the hor — ' the man started, but his words were cut short when Slim delivered a powerful back-handed slap across his face.

'What happened?' Slim asked again.

The man tasted blood at the corner

of his mouth and his eyes started to fill with tears.

'The sheriff will kill me,' the man said. 'If I talk I'm dead.'

Slim pushed his gun forward, pressing the cruel eye into the man's forehead so tightly that when he eased off it left an indentation in the man's flesh.

'I'll kill you if you don't,' Slim said.

'What do you want me to say?' Hayes asked, his eyes going from Slim to Blackman. 'What can I say?'

'Start with the truth,' Slim said. 'Who killed the deputy?'

'Deke.'

'The sheriff?'

Hayes nodded. 'Yeah, the sheriff,' he said.

'Why?' Slim prodded the man with the gun to remind him that it was there.

'John Conner was a good man,' Hayes said.

'Conner? That the deputy?'

Again Hayes nodded.

Slim frowned. Now that the deputy

had a name it made his killing all the more real. It was one thing being blamed for the killing of an anonymous lawman, but now that the dead man had been given an identity, it was doubly troubling. There was no way Slim was going to allow his gun to be attributed to the killing of the deputy.

'He wasn't supposed to be in town,' Hayes said. 'He'd been out serving warrants and wasn't expected back to town for a day or two. He had no idea what was going on until the sheriff plugged him. It was a dirty and cowardly way to kill a man.'

'What was going on? Why did the sheriff kill his man?'

'I don't know,' Hayes said and then held up a hand when it looked as if Slim was going to slap him again. 'Look, all I know is that Deke was into something with McBain.'

'McBain?'

'The bank owner,' Hayes explained. 'I don't know exactly what dirty dealings the two men are involved in, only that it involves money, a lot of money. Deputy Conner was on to them, and, of course, he'd likely contradict the sheriff's story about you boys storming his office, so the sheriff likely felt killing Conner was the safest option.'

'You saw the sheriff shoot him?' Blackman asked, leaning over Slim to catch Hayes's frightened eyes.

Hayes nodded.

'I didn't know that's what he was fixin' to do, though,' he said. 'Not until it was too late. As soon as you boys rode out of town I went over to Deke's office. I discovered both men were tied up, the sheriff was also shackled, and I released them. The sheriff shot Conner almost immediately and then forced me to go along with whatever he said. I had no choice.'

'There's always a choice,' Slim said, mulling over everything the man had told him.

'Maybe for men like you,' Hayes said, 'but not for the likes of me. I felt bad for the deputy, but what could I do?

The sheriff'll kill me without any hesitation and what's more he'd take pleasure in doing so.'

'Someone's coming,' Tanner suddenly shouted from the doorway.

Blackman turned on his feet and went to the doorway, peering outside. Sure enough a man was crossing the street, leading his horse towards the stable. The man was carrying a lot of trail dust on both himself and his clothing.

'I think some dude wants to stable his horse,' Blackman shouted back to Slim. 'Looks like he's just gotten into town.'

Slim lifted Hayes to his feet and then poked his Colt against the fat of the man's stomach.

'When the man comes in here,' Slim said. 'Just go about your business as usual. Try any tricks and you get it first.'

Hayes nodded.

'Yes, sir,' he said. 'No tricks.'

'Get your horses into stalls,' Slim said to his two friends and then led his own horse into an empty stall while Hayes picked up his sweeping brush and started to brush the floor. He was shaking visibly and Slim smiled, thinking it was not likely that Hayes would try anything; he was far too scared for that.

A moment later a man popped his head around the doorway and looked at each of the men in turn.

'Who is in charge here?' the man asked.

'I am,' Hayes said, and walked to the newcomer. He held out a hand, which the man took. 'Samuel C. Hayes at your service.'

The man shook the offered hand and smiled.

'I'd like to stable my horse,' the man said. 'Get it fed and watered.'

'Sure thing,' Hayes said and took the reins from the man. He pulled the horse, a handsome looking paint, and led it to a free stall. 'That's my business.'

'Could he get a brush down?' the man asked.

'Sure,' Hayes said. 'It's all in with the price.'

'And check his shoes,' the man said. 'We've covered many miles and I don't want him going lame on me.'

'You bet,' Hayes said.

'You here on business, stranger?' Slim asked, emerging from the stall where he had been seeing to his own horse.

The man looked at Slim for a moment before answering, and both Blackman and Tanner froze, expecting trouble but there was none forthcoming and instead the man smiled warmly.

'I've been on the trail for weeks,' he said. 'I've got a few more miles ahead of me but I thought it'd be nice to get a warm meal and sleep in a soft bed.'

'Where you heading?' Slim asked, making small talk. He could see that Hayes was shaking and he was glad when the man went into the stall with the newcomer's horse.

'Kansas,' the man said. 'My pa's got a ranch there.'

'Never been there,' Slim said. 'Would

like to one day.'

'You should,' the man said and dusted himself down. 'Anyway what do I owe for the horse?'

'You can pay when you collect him,' Hayes said, speaking over the top of the stall. 'Prices are all on the board up there.' He pointed to a chalkboard besides the stable entrance.

'Obliged,' the newcomer said and tipped his hat before leaving the stable in search of the hotel, a warm meal and a bath.

'You did real good,' Slim said and grabbed Hayes by the scruff of the neck and pulled him from the stall. 'Can you read and write?' Slim asked.

Hayes looked confused, which was something he had in common with both Tanner and Blackman.

'Write,' Slim said. 'Can you write?'

'I'm lettered,' Hayes said, looking more confused than ever.

'Good,' Slim said. 'You got anything to write on in your office?'

'Yes,' Hayes said.

'Then come on.' Slim dragged the man across the stable and into the office at the rear of the building.

Tanner and Blackman exchanged a puzzled glance and then followed Slim and Hayes to the office. They knew that one of them should have kept watch at the entrance to the stables, but they were both intrigued to see just what Slim had in mind for Hayes.

Hayes sat behind his desk and removed a large sheet of paper from the one and only drawer. The paper was headed, Hope Springs Livery & Grain. He picked up a stubby pencil from his desk, licked the end, and held it over the paper, poised to write. He looked at Slim, his expression one big question.

'The deputy,' Slim said. 'The deputy the sheriff, killed. The newspaper said he left a widow.'

Hayes nodded.

'She lives out in Douglas Valley,' he said. 'Conner built their place himself.'

'Then start with your name,' Slim said. 'And then address the letter to the widow. I want you to tell her what really happened to her husband. Everything, put down everything you can remember and make sure you mention the involvement of that banker.'

Hayes looked at each of the men in turn, hand poised over the still blank piece of paper.

'Write or I'll shoot you down like a dog,' Slim said. 'I'll shoot you here and now.'

Hayes started to write.

'Will one of you two keep watch?' Slim asked and smiled when Tanner went back to the doorway. He walked behind Hayes and looked down, reading over his shoulder.

'Just what have you got in mind?' Blackman asked, feeling that he wasn't going to like the answer.

9

Blackman sat there beside the fire smoking a quirly while Tanner, curled up on the ground with a horse blanket wrapped around him, alternately snored and smacked his lips together. Blackman never failed to be amazed at the way his old friend managed to sleep at all given the almighty ruckus he made while doing so.

The horses, Slim's body still tied to one of them, were tethered to the branches of a gnarled oak tree behind them. The horses were shielded from view by the thick scrub around them.

The two men had set up camp for the night in the small clearing in the middle of a woodland that was dense with deciduous trees, herbaceous shrubs and evergreens. The woodland floor was covered with cottonweed, which grew in clumps several feet wide. They had set up here because the woodlands sheltered them and although the weather was fairly clement for the time of year, they both knew that things could change mighty quickly.

Camping there also gave them the security of being virtually invisible to anyone riding the rough mountain trails above them. And although they were both starting to relax as far as possible posses were concerned, they had learned from past experience that it was better to take precautions against being caught unawares.

There were too many potential dangers out there to ever grow lax.

Blackman finished his smoke and flicked the remains into the fire. Kept low the flames hungrily accepted the cigarette stub and Blackman immediately lit another. He cast a glance over his shoulder, peering through the tree-line, picking out the vague outline of Slim upon the horse and smiled.

'Good to have you back with us,' he mumbled and gave the corpse the thumbs up.

Blackman had the sack containing their sizeable fortune on his blanket beside him and he squeezed it, as though wanting to verify that the money was indeed in there, that he hadn't imagined all this. $59,000 — it was their biggest haul ever and the irony of Slim being involved in his most lucrative bank robbery many years after his death, wasn't lost on the old man. He guessed that if things went well, and they managed to escape whatever law was after them, they would disappear to spend the rest of their lives in comfort. The legend of Slim McCord would grow beyond all proportion if they managed to vanish without trace. There would be those who believed that Slim had returned from the grave in order to secure one last haul, and Blackman felt mighty good about it.

The world needed stories like that.

Blackman thought of Slim and all he had meant to him, and the fact that his old friend's remains were here sharing the trail gave him great comfort. It had been unsettling to ride into Possum Creek and find the body of their old friend on show in that carny tent. It had seemed the kind of unlikely event that never really happened in life and was reserved solely for tall tales told around the camp-fire. Just like the tall tales that people would tell of how Slim had returned from the grave, and robbed the Possum Creek bank of an absolute fortune and all without a shot being fired. And whilst that may not be strictly true, strange things had happened.

Blackman felt that it was fate, that it had all somehow been preordained, that he and Tanner had been meant to ride into that town and discover the mummified remains of their old friend. That it had been some supernatural interference that had made the bank manager drop the key, that Slim had somehow influenced events to the extent of ensuring the amount of money in the bank's safe.

Blackman and Tanner hadn't been

with Slim when he had been killed in Santino, but had heard about the event from a group of settlers they had met up with in California. The death of a notable outlaw, and Slim was indeed notable, was the kind of news that spread around the country like wildfire. It would travel from person to person and then seem to jump from town to town, territory to territory, state to state, and even to other countries, travelling across land and ocean. That kind of news spread so quickly that it was soon ahead of itself, and no sooner would someone ride into some desolate one horse town on the edge of nowhere, aching to share the news, than they would discover the news had gotten there before them. The modern wonder of the telegraph was put to shame by word of mouth among the Western network of drifting cowboys.

They hadn't seen Slim for more than three years when they'd heard he had been killed. They had separated a few years previously when Slim managed to slip past the posse that he and Tanner had not managed to evade. All the law could pin on Blackman and Tanner was a stage robbery, so they had been given fifteen months hard labour in a hellhole the authorities called a correctional facility. They had always intended to meet back up with Slim when they were paroled, but fate had decreed otherwise and a few months after Blackman and Tanner had found themselves free men they had heard of their old friend's death; *shot in the back by a lawman in Santino*.

The next time they would see Slim would prove to be as a mummified exhibit at the travelling carny show.

Blackman spat into the fire, watching it hiss as it found the hot coals and then finished his cigarette and tossed that into the smouldering coals. He stood up, stretching to relieve a cramp and decided he'd fix himself some coffee before trying to get a few hours' shuteye. The pot was empty and so Blackman pushed through the trees to his horse and collected his canteen and a bag of Folgers from his saddle-bags.

'Gonna find you somewhere real nice to rest,' Blackman said, pausing to talk to his old friend's remains. 'Somewhere real nice, where the sun catches your grave in the morning. We made a good haul this time, our biggest ever, and me and Tanner are gonna end our days like kings.'

Blackman fell silent for a moment, as though waiting for Slim to reply.

'We sure do wish you were here to enjoy it,' Blackman said. 'But, hell, you're with us on this trail, I know it, I can feel it. We rode together a long time, Slim, and we, I know I speak for Tanner, looked to you like a brother, our elder brother. We may not have been blood but each of us would spill it for the other.'

Again Blackman paused, as though waiting for Slim to reply.

'We'll come by your grave,' he continued. 'Every so often we'll come by and place a flower against your marker, tell you how things are going. It'll be good to do that. I'd like to do that.'

With that Blackman fell silent. He stood there with Slim for a moment but then pushed back through the trees to sit back down beside the fire. Tanner was still snoring away, not even aware that his friend had gone and then returned and he continued to sleep as Blackman poured the contents of his canteen into the pot and then tipped in a few scoops of Folgers, sat back and he waited for the coffee to boil.

He rolled himself another quirly and then froze when he heard a sound from somewhere in the darkness. He remained perfectly still, listening, a hand hovering over the butt of his Colt but other than the usual night sounds there was nothing to be heard.

'You're getting jumpy, old man,' Blackman scolded himself and stuck the quirly into his mouth. He reached out and grabbed the coffee pot and then poured a helping of the thick liquid into a tin coffee cup.

He heard it again.

That time there was no mistaking the sound: a twig snapping underfoot.

And now the horses had sensed someone was nearby and they grew restless, stomping and snorting.

Blackman got to his feet, filled his hand and turned, peering into the darkness of the tree line, while Tanner, oblivious to all but his dreams, slept on. For a moment Blackman could see nothing but sheer darkness, but then there was a sudden flash of movement and before Blackman could get a shot off he found himself pushed to the ground, an Indian brave, seeming to appear out of thin air, was upon him, a lethal-looking knife held to his throat. Blackman struggled but the knife bit against his flesh and he held himself still, staring up at the cat-like eyes of the Indian.

Tanner came awake suddenly but his words were cut short by a hand clamping over his mouth as a second

Indian put in an appearance. Tanner felt a knife held to his own throat and his frightened eyes found Blackman's.

Indians, Blackman thought. Only Indians could be so fast, get so close without being seen and for a moment he thought there may be more hiding out there in the darkness, but after several seconds with no further movement he figured that these two braves were alone. Not that it made much difference since they had the drop on them and could quite easily kill them, which was likely what the two of them had in mind. Although the years of Indian troubles across the West had gone into the history pages, there were still small flare-ups from time to time. Even Geronimo, Blackman had heard, had surrendered some years back and now travelled around with one of those Wild West shows, but none of that mattered since these two braves seemed very much at war with the whites.

'What are you men doing out here?' the Indian holding Blackman asked as he removed his hand from the man's mouth.

'You speak English,' Blackman stated the obvious.

'What are you doing here?' the Indian repeated while his partner kept hold of Tanner who had stopped struggling since the knife at his throat had nicked him. A thin trickle of blood ran down Tanner's shirtfront.

'We ain't doing nothing,' Blackman said. 'Just travelling is all.'

'Where you go?' the Indian asked.

'We go nowhere in particular,' Blackman said. 'We just go.'

'You look for yellow stones?' the Indian asked.

Momentarily Blackman was confused but then it dawned on him. Yellow stones! The Indian thought they were gold prospectors. At once he understood the Indian's hostility as he himself had seen prospectors trampling over sacred burial grounds with gold fever in their eyes.

'No,' Blackman said. 'We just go.'

'All white men look for yellow stones,' the Indian said. 'White man look everywhere. Inside mountains. On sacred ground. You will die.'

Blackman struggled again, hoping to catch the brave unawares, but it was to no avail and the Indian held him tight. The braves were much younger than either he or Tanner and were having no trouble holding them. He felt the knife tightening across his throat and he gritted his teeth, preparing to meet his Maker.

Suddenly one of their horses broke free and found its way into the clearing.

Both of the Indians released the men and stood up, dropping their knives to the ground as they stared at the dead man riding the horse towards them. One of them let out a fierce yell of terror and then both he and his companion vanished into the woods. The two men forgotten, the Indians could be heard crashing through the woodland and eventually they heard the sound of galloping ponies, until once more silence resumed.

Blackman ran a hand over his throat and then stood up. He looked at Tanner who was wide eyed in shock and seemed unable to get to his feet. Then he cast his eyes towards the horse and Slim tied to its back.

'He saved us,' Blackman said. 'Slim saved us again.'

Tanner finally managed to get up. He felt the blood trickling down his throat and realized just how close he had been to death.

'Indians,' Tanner said. 'I hate Indians.'

'Guess we weren't too popular with them neither,' Blackman said and grabbed the reins of the horse holding Slim's remains. He looked up at the body of his old friend and mouthed a silent 'thank you', for the man had no doubt that it was Slim's intervention here that had saved both himself and Tanner from certain death.

Tanner grabbed his makings and with shaking hands managed to put together a quirly. He placed it in his mouth and took a match to it, feeling the tobacco immediately calming his shaken nerves.

'I ain't staying here no longer,' Tanner said. 'I've had enough camp for one night. Let's move on.'

Blackman nodded and led the horse carrying Slim back to the others.

10

'Guess we know what happened to that writer's horse,' Baxter said as he gently ran his fingertips over the ground. It was not long after dawn and there was still dew on the ground, which told Baxter that the tracks had been left sometime yesterday since several of the indentations had acted as dew-traps.

They had first picked up on the two riders' tracks some miles back, and followed them into the mountains, before having to set up camp for the night. With morning light they had soon rediscovered the trail, but now they had come upon an extra set of tracks. Another horse, but the strange thing was that at times each of the horses seemed to be carrying a rider, and at others one of the horses left shallow tracks as though it were carrying nothing upon its back.

'You still think it's two men?' the deputy asked, and cast a glance back at the rest of the posse.

Baxter nodded, and looked at Rawlings.

'We're after two men. Of that I'm certain.'

'So what's the trouble?'

'It's this third horse,' Baxter said. 'Likely the beast that writer had run off on him.'

'What about it?'

'It's strange,' Baxter said. 'But at times it leaves tracks as if it's carrying a rider and then others it looks to be riderless.'

'So?'

'So,' Baxter said, 'it just don't make no sense, is all.'

'Maybe they loaded the horse up with provisions,' the deputy suggested. 'That kind of uneven weight could leave tracks like that.'

Baxter spat into the dirt and looked up into the mountains, wondering who it was ahead of them. He shook his head, figuring it didn't really matter since they would find out soon enough. Of that he was sure. There wasn't a man or beast that Clem Baxter couldn't track down.

'How far ahead?' Deputy Rawlings asked, putting together a smoke from the makings he'd taken from his shirt pocket. Following his lead several other men in the posse started putting smokes together.

'A day,' Baxter said, jumping back into the saddle. 'Maybe a little more.'

'Then let's move on,' the deputy said. 'We'll get a good deal higher into the mountains before we take a break.'

And with that the posse continued up the mountain pass, negotiating some tricky, barely passable terrain as they went higher into the mountainous range.

* * *

Tanner couldn't stop thinking of the Indian attack of the previous night. He sat uneasily in the saddle, his eyes frightened and darting about in his head. They would have to go some way before he would feel safe again. Not only did they have a posse behind them, and with a haul of more than $50,000 they were sure there would be a posse in pursuit and a damn good one at that, but there was also the very real possibility that they were, even at this very moment, surrounded by unseen Indians.

It was getting colder too. The higher they went the more the temperature dropped, and although Tanner trusted his friend he sure wished they had taken a different route away from Possum Creek. The mountain pass, Blackman had insisted, was the best and safest way into the next state. It would make it harder for the law to follow them and offered them a better chance of passing through the territory unseen, since few folk travelled the mountains now that the railroads and wagon trails ran across the plains below them.

That much may have been true but Tanner figured that at least they'd be able to see any Indians coming out on the plains. He'd had many experiences with Indians over the years, and none of them had been particularly pleasant. The fact that Tanner had been trespassing across sacred grounds, or violating one treaty or another, when the Indians had turned on him, mattered little to the old man. He didn't trust Indians and didn't feel safe anywhere near them. It was true that the Indian Wars were long over and that there was seldom trouble these days, but all the same Tanner was too long in the tooth to change his opinion. There were those who claimed that the whites and the Indians would live in harmony one day but Tanner doubted it. He'd been around when the white men and the red men had been mortal enemies, and his opinions and prejudices, which had been built up over a long lifetime, were not going to change anytime soon.

'We should maybe stop,' Tanner said.

'Rest the horses and maybe take some food.'

Blackman looked back over his shoulder at his companion, who was riding behind the horse carrying Slim's body. They were all moving at the same steady pace and both men were bone weary of the excitement of the previous night.

'I figure we'll go a little higher first,' Blackman said. 'The mountain's starting to level out and I don't think we're far from the summit. Maybe another day and we'll be heading down into the Black Valleys and then there ain't a posse that'll be able to track us.'

'You think the posse is far behind?' Tanner asked.

'Don't know,' Blackman said. 'We ain't caught a sight of them but they must be after us. I reckon we gained a good advantage with our head start so it would be foolish for us to waste that advantage and not keep moving. We don't want to give them too much of a chance to catch up.'

'Figure so,' Tanner said grudgingly. He had to admit that his friend was making perfect sense, but it was the Indians who worried him far more than a posse, and he feared that where there were two Indians there could be a heap more.

Above them a buzzard drifted on the wind which troubled Tanner even more. He was sure the buzzard had sensed death, their death and was sticking with them in order to take a feast on their remains.

'If there's one thing I hate more than Indians it's buzzards,' Tanner said, more to himself than his companion.

Blackman looked up at the sky and saw the buzzard circling. It cast an ominous shadow as it went between them and the sun and despite the fact that he wasn't as easily spooked as Tanner, he too found the predator's presence unsettling. Maybe there was something dead around here that was attracting the bird, Blackman thought. He wondered if the bird was following them because of Slim. Though he knew that couldn't be so because Slim had been preserved, with his innards removed and his belly full of sawdust, so there was nothing there to draw the attention of the buzzard.

'Darn buzzard,' Tanner complained.

'If any buzzard bites you it'll never eat flesh again,' Blackman retorted.

Ahead of them the trees began to thin out until they found themselves in another clearing. There was a stream of crystal-clear water a few yards in front of them and both men dismounted and led their horses to the stream so that they could take a drink. Slim's horse, still tied to the saddle of Blackman's horse, made its own way to the water's edge and greedily drunk from the stream.

'Let them take their fill,' Blackman said. 'We'll go on for a few hours yet before stopping.'

Tanner nodded and took his makings from his pocket.

'I suppose we could ride till noon,' he

said, rolling himself a quirly.

'That would seem the sensible thing to do.' Blackman also removed his makings and quickly put together a quirly.

'I'm sure as hell feeling my age now,' Tanner said, a cloud of smoke escaping between his teeth as he spoke.

'I guess I am too,' Blackman admitted. 'Well we've got enough money now to see our days out, so I guess this'll be our last great adventure. We'll bury Slim and then vanish, get us a small place and a couple of rocking chairs.'

Tanner smiled. That sounded so good to him.

'We'll sit in those chairs from sunup to sundown,' he said.

'We can sure afford to now.'

'Fifty thousand dollars,' Tanner said, looking at the saddle-bags that hung over Blackman's horse.

'Fifty nine thousand,' Blackman corrected him.

A silence fell between them while they both finished their smokes and once that was done, they flicked their stubs on to the ground and then both mounted their horses. Tanner looked at the sky above them and was pleased to see that the buzzard had moved on.

'Let's go get our rocking chairs,' Blackman said, and spurred his horse onwards.

★　★　★

Yesteryear

Slim pulled his horse to a stop and looked down from the rise to the small house on the valley floor below. Smoke drifted lazily from the chimney and for a moment Slim could picture the woman in there, her children wrapped in her arms while they huddled around the fire.

Slim suddenly felt nervous and for the briefest of moments, he considered turning around and going back to town where Tanner and Blackman waited in the livery stable with Hayes, but he knew what had to be done, what he had to do.

He gently sent his horse off down into the valley.

When he had decided on this course of action it had seemed the thing to do, but now Slim wasn't so sure. He didn't know how the woman would react to him and there was the possibility that she wouldn't believe the words Hayes had written.

What if she went for a gun?

A woman alone with two children would surely have a gun somewhere around the place.

Slim ignored the thoughts, knowing that he had to do what he had to do. It was as simple as that and no matter how this played out, he would be able to ride away with a clean conscience. He would present the woman with the letter and the $2,000, minus the $300, he carried in his saddle-bags. Once that was done he would return to town, collect his two friends and ride as far away as possible from Hope Springs.

It was the right thing to do.

The only thing to do.

150

Blackman and Tanner hadn't been happy with his plan and thought he was loco. Tanner even went so far as to inform him of that fact, but Slim had argued his case, told them that it wasn't only him who was being blamed for murdering the deputy, leaving the woman without a husband and the children without a father. Both men had tried to talk Slim out of it, but his mind had been made up and there was no way he was going to be dissuaded.

Blackman had said that he and Tanner should come along, but Slim told them they had to keep an eye on Hayes. If the man ran to the sheriff as soon as they were gone it seemed likely the sheriff would come out to the widow's place after them, and that was something Slim didn't want. Then it was suggested that Hayes be taken with them, but Slim figured and argued that they would be more likely to be seen, and the alarm sounded if they dragged Hayes along.

The only way to do this was for Slim

to ride out alone, present the widow with the money and letter and then ride back so that they could all skedaddle before the widow took the letter to the proper authorities. The army were only stationed twenty miles away and if the widow took the letter to them, then it was pretty likely that a troop would ride into Hope Springs and place the sheriff and banker under military arrest, thus clearing the name of Slim McCord and the so-called vicious killers he rode with. It was the only way, Slim claimed, to prevent bloodshed, which was something none of the men wanted.

Slim reached the valley floor and again had to fight off the compulsion to turn and flee. He reminded himself of the deputy, of how he was being blamed for the murder. He didn't want to gain the reputation of a killer. Not only was killing a hanging offence but it was not something Slim McCord wanted to be associated with. Yes, he had killed in the past, but only because there had been no other way. Slim didn't like killing and even when the act was justified, he suffered pangs of remorse that would return from time to time to haunt his sleep. Men he had killed years back still lived in his dreams.

Slim McCord was many things but he was most certainly not a killer.

It was a hell of a thing to kill a man. Killing took away anything the man was and anything he had the potential to be.

At the valley floor, Slim set his horse off into a trot towards the small house. There was a low fence around the house with a hinged gate in the centre and, as Slim reached the gate, he saw the front door open and a woman, the widow most likely, emerge from the doorway. She paused to take a look at Slim and then stepped out as a tall black man, carrying a shotgun pushed his way past her and onto the front step.

'Who are you stranger?' the man asked and the woman came and stood beside him. There were two children, a boy and girl, standing just inside the doorway and they both seemed scared, unsure of the situation.

'I didn't come for trouble,' Slim said. 'I came with some information.'

'That's not what I asked,' the man said. 'I asked who you were.'

'Are you the Widow Conner?' Slim directed his question at the woman, ignoring the man.

'I am.'

'And I'm Jake Riley,' the man said. 'Now who the hell are you, stranger?'

Slim looked first at the woman and then at the two children in the doorway.

'I prefer to talk without those two children around,' he said.

'Mister,' Riley said. 'I don't know who you are but that's not very polite and I think you're frightening Mrs Conner and the children. Now turn around and ride away or I'll use this here gun.'

'No, Jake.' The woman placed a hand on the man's shoulder. She looked at Slim and felt that there was something in his eyes that she could trust. She should at least hear what he had to say, whoever he was. 'Would you care to come in, Mr . . . er?'

'McCord,' Slim said and noticed the reaction the name got.

The woman's eyes widened slightly while Riley's face filled with fury.

'I'd just as soon talk out here,' Slim said.

The woman turned and told the children to wait inside, close the door. When the children had done so she turned back to Slim.

'McCord is the name of the man who killed my husband,' she said.

'I know,' Slim said. 'I'm the man being blamed for killing him. I didn't, though.'

'Mister,' Riley said, 'I don't know what this is, what you think you are doing, but you've taken a risk to come here. The law are out looking for you and if I shot you dead here and now I'd likely get a medal for my trouble.'

'A reward at least,' Slim said. 'But that don't change the fact that I didn't kill no deputy.'

The woman looked at Slim. She didn't know what to do but she was surprised to find that she felt no fear. Nor was there hatred for this man whom they said had killed her husband in cold blood. If it were true, that he had killed her husband then there was no sense in him being here like this. He wore guns but hadn't made a move towards them despite the fact that Jake was holding a shotgun on him.

'I'm gonna count to three,' Jake said, 'and if you're not riding away I'm gonna pull this trigger.'

'No.' The woman pushed his shotgun so that it was pointed at the ground. 'Let him speak.'

'Thank you,' Slim said, and slowly, so as not to spook either of them, climbed down from the saddle. He stood there, looking at the man and woman, his arms held at his side but well away from his guns.

'Then speak,' Jake prompted, but kept his own weapon towards the ground.

'Firstly, I'm sorry to hear of your loss,' Slim said, 'but I didn't kill your husband.'

'Then who the hell did?' Jake snapped and momentarily raised and then lowered the shotgun when Slim didn't move for his own guns.

'The sheriff,' Slim said, noticing something in the widow's eyes but not sure exactly what. It wasn't shock and could have been a realization of sorts. Whatever the look had been it was quite obviously not total disbelief.

'Sheriff Caxton,' she said. 'Why would he?'

'I'm not sure of the details,' Slim said. 'But I have something for you that may help. I need to reach into my shirt so I hope you don't get shaky with that there cannon,' Slim directed the last part of his speech at Riley.

'Go on, stranger,' Riley said, but now he held the gun aimed at Slim once more. 'Move slowly. My finger may stumble on this here trigger if there's any sudden moves.'

Slowly Slim reached into his shirt and pulled out the letter Hayes had written back in the livery stable. He took several steps towards the widow and then held out the letter, and she took it.

'I've also brought you this,' Slim said, and once again he reached into his shirt and pulled out a small bundle wrapped in newspaper. He tossed it onto the ground.

'What's that?' Jake asked.

'Two thousand dollars,' Slim said. 'It's the money we robbed from the sheriff. Figure your needs are more than ours.' The fact Slim had promised Blackman and Tanner that he would hold back $300 didn't enter his mind. He wanted the widow to have the money, felt it was rightfully hers. It was not a substitute for a husband to care for her and the children, but it would certainly make things a little easier in the short term.

The woman finally looked up from the letter. Her face had drained of all colour and there were tears in the corner of her eyes.

'This is the truth?' she asked.

'Every word,' Slim said. 'I think it was all a set up for the sheriff to explain the missing money. That two thousand is all we took and when we left that deputy, your husband, was very much alive. Hayes, the fella who wrote that there letter, witnessed the killing of your husband.'

The woman turned to Jake and handed him the letter, which he took and quickly read.

'I want you to watch the children,' she said.

'What?' Riley looked up from the letter. He no longer held the shotgun in a threatening manner but rested it beneath an arm.

'I'm going into town with Mr McCord,' she said, and then turned to Slim. 'You are going back into town?'

'I am,' Slim said. 'But I don't think it's wise you coming along. You just take that there letter to the army. Let them bring this sheriff to justice.'

'That's what I aim to do,' the widow said. 'But I need to talk to this man Hayes first. I'll go alone if I have to.'

Slim frowned.

'I don't plan on coming back here,' Slim said. 'It could be too dangerous. If the sheriff finds out what's happening he'll do anything to get that letter and destroy it. He'll kill anyone in his way. That's what a cornered rat usually does.'

'I'm coming into town,' the woman said. 'I'll go with you or without you.'

Slim admired her spunk.

'I'll take you in,' he said. 'You speak to Hayes and me and my men will bring you back, but then we're gone.'

The woman nodded, bent and picked up the bundle of money and handed it to Riley.

'Put this safe, Jake,' she said. 'Watch the children until I return.'

'You don't know this man,' he protested. 'He could be fixin' to do anything.'

'You've read the letter,' the woman retorted.

He nodded. 'I have.'

'I believe him.' The widow spoke in a gentle tone of voice. 'If he had killed John then why go to this charade? What is there to gain from coming here? If he had done the killing then I doubt he, or his men, would be anywhere near this place. I'm going into town and I'm speaking with this Hayes. I want to know what really happened.'

Slim couldn't help but admire her. Her strength of character was plainly obvious and she was no fool.

'You're gonna be the death of me,' Riley said and then smiled at her. He turned to Slim and his face took on a harder edge. 'You get her back here,' he said, 'or I'll hunt you down and kill you. No matter how long it takes I'll kill you.'

'I believe you would,' Slim said. 'I believe you would.'

11

They had long passed the summit, and were heading into the Black Valleys when they decided to make camp for the night. They were fast losing light, the horizon had turned a vivid red, and to continue now was to risk injury to themselves or the horses. Blackman would have preferred to cover a few more miles before nightfall, to at least have entered the valleys, but he knew it made more sense to make camp here. And besides, he reasoned, they had travelled a good distance today, only taking the one break around noon and that hadn't been for longer than an hour, so it was a good bet they had put even further distance between them and any possible posse in pursuit.

Both men, like their horses, were bone weary.

The Black Valleys, so called because

of the gritstone cliff walls, went on west as far as the eye could see and the two men knew that they had three to four days of hell ahead of them before coming to the Chaytor River and the more hospitable land beyond. After that, and assuming a posse hadn't put in an appearance by then, they figured they would be safe and could find somewhere suitable to bury Slim before vanishing and finding a nice quiet town within which to live out the rest of their lives.

For now though they needed to rest if they were to have the strength for the still arduous journey that lay ahead of them.

'Reckon we could try and rustle up something other than jerky,' Tanner said. 'Maybe a wild turkey or a jack-rabbit. Even a rattler would taste mighty good about now.'

'You do that,' Blackman said. 'I'll set us a small fire.'

Tanner nodded and dismounted. He reached into his saddle-bags and took out a piece of string with which to make a small noose, and then took a look at Slim. He guessed the events of the past few days were getting to him because for a moment he was sure he'd seen Slim smile at him.

'I'll go catch us something,' he said.

'Be careful,'

'Loco,' Tanner vanished into the scrub, leaving Blackman to fix the camp-fire.

★ ★ ★

Tanner didn't have to roam too far from the camp before coming across a likely looking burrow. He snapped a lengthy, though thin branch from a nearby softwood tree and poked it into the burrow, shaking it about to disturb any occupants. Then he lay himself down on the ground, but out of view of the burrow's entrance and hung the noose end of the string so that it could be pulled tight on any emerging critter.

Then Tanner waited patiently.

He had done this before and knew from past experience that it wasn't usually too long before some curious critter would come out to investigate, and end up in the cooking pot for its troubles. For the past few days they had eaten nothing but grits and jerky and fresh meat would go down a treat right about now, and so Tanner lay there and waited.

He was nodding off when he heard the scratching coming from within the burrow. He snapped instantly alert and tensed, ready to pull the noose closed when the critter put in its appearance. It took a few more minutes and the man was just about to give up when the jack-rabbit, a bulky white-tailed creature, poked its head out of the burrow and through the noose which Tanner immediately pulled tight, taking the startled creature off its feet and into the air. The man quickly killed it with his knife and then held it up by its hind legs, feeling his stomach already starting to rumble in anticipation.

'Sorry, critter,' he said to the rabbit. 'But I'm sure gonna enjoy eating you.'

Tanner started back towards the camp, feeling elated now that he had the makings of a tasty supper. The rabbit was big enough for a fine stew, which meant that tonight they would be able to sleep with full stomachs and have enough of the meat left over to set them off for another long ride come morning.

Tanner was pleased to find that his partner had already got the fire going and was boiling a pot of coffee which sent off a delicious aroma onto the evening air. The horses, Slim still tied to his, were tethered to various branches.

'Get your skinning knife,' Tanner said and tossed the jack-rabbit onto the ground next to Blackman.

Blackman looked first at the jack-rabbit and then flicked the remains of the cigarette he had been smoking into the fire.

'Yes, sir,' he answered with a smirk.

Afterwards they both sat around the

small fire, smoking cigarettes and drinking strong coffee. The aftertaste of their meal lingered in their mouths and for the first time in many days the two men felt comfortable. They sat there in silence and watched the sky as the vivid red of dusk was replaced by the inky blackness of night.

* * *

Deputy Rawlings tipped the dregs of his coffee into the fire and stretched to work a kink out of his back. He looked at his men — Baxter was sitting, chewing the last of the meat from a thick bone while the other four men — Glover, Teeks, Wilson and Riggs — were seated around the camp-fire and sharing a bottle of whiskey.

'Don't drink too much of that,' Rawlings said, as he walked past the men and made his way to Baxter. The deputy would have preferred the man didn't partake in strong spirits at all while they were on the trail of the outlaws, but they were simple townsfolk and were only here because of civic duty, so he allowed them their little pleasures. There was no harm in it, but all the same he would keep a close eye on them and if any of them appeared too drunk to be useful, or worse, to become a liability, he would leave them behind and tell them to make their way back to Possum Creek.

Baxter looked up as the deputy approached him. He was now chewing on a clay pipe, having set the bone aside and the smoke escaped from the corners of his mouth in thin trickles.

'I'm figuring we ride on in maybe an hour,' Rawlings said and sat himself down on the ground besides the man.

'I can't track in the dark,' Baxter said.

'No matter.' Rawlings took his own makings from the pouch tucked into his gunbelt and quickly put together a quirly. 'We know the way they're heading and I figure that if we don't do a little catch up we'll lose them altogether.'

Baxter nodded.

'That could be so,' he said. A few miles back they had come across the remains of a fire that was no more than a day old, so they were at least gaining on their quarry.

'If we lose them,' the deputy said, 'then we can try to pick up their trail, but if not then so be it. We're sure enough gonna lose them if we don't shorten the distance between them and us.'

'Guess so.'

'Good,' Rawlings drew deeply on his quirly. 'Reckon I'll tell the men.'

Baxter nodded, said nothing more and went back to his pipe and the burley mix.

Rawlings sat there for sometime in silence while he smoked. He figured the outlaws were looking to escape into the Black Valleys, and he feared that if they reached them before the posse had even caught sight of them, they would be gone forever. That wouldn't make Sheriff Caxton happy, not with them outlaws having escaped with such a large haul. Of course, the fact that the outlaws had gained such a head start on the posse didn't help at all.

Whoever the outlaws were, the deputy figured, they were a highly skilled duo. They had gotten in and out of the bank with no sign of how they had done it. In fact the only reason their crime had been discovered was because of the missing money. There was something strange about that and the deputy was convinced the sheriff knew more about the whole affair than he was letting on. There had been something in Caxton's face when the deputy had questioned him about the details of the robbery, but all the sheriff would say was that someone had gotten into the bank, cracked the safe and then got out again. It was mighty strange.

Made even stranger still by the fact that whoever the outlaws were they had also stolen the mummified remains of Slim McCord, a man who in his day had been a famous outlaw himself.

Now why was that?

What the hell did a group of outlaws want with the body of a long dead outlaw?

Rawlings finished his smoke and shook his head. There was no use thinking about it, since it all sounded too crazy to make any kind of sense. A bank robbery with no sign of entry, a top quality safe opened as though with the combination and a mummified outlaw. The deputy guessed that he would only really get the answers to all the questions when they caught up with the two outlaws.

'We're riding out in a half-hour,' he shouted, and made his way over to his horse. He ignored the groans coming from the four men sat around the fire and instead busied himself with getting his horse ready for the night ride.

★　★　★

Yesteryear
Sheriff Dawkins did a double take.

He couldn't believe what he was seeing.

There was that man Slim McCord, bold as brass walking down the main street with a woman who, even from this distance the sheriff could see was the Widow Conner.

What was happening here?

The sheriff didn't like this one little bit.

Slim and the widow were unaware that the sheriff was watching them as they went into the livery stable, and once inside they were greeted by Blackman and Tanner who were standing watching Hayes as the old man swept out a stall. They both turned when Slim entered, as did the old man who put his sweeping brush aside and looked at the widow.

'Are these words true?' Widow Conner asked, holding the letter Hayes had written not an hour ago.

Hayes nodded.

'Afraid so,' he said and directed his eyes down to the floor. 'I'm sorry but there was nothing I could do. The sheriff would have killed me without hesitation.'

The widow's eyes became tearful and she had to fight back a sob. Slim, standing beside her, placed an arm on one of her shoulders and gave her a smile of support.

'You need to take that there letter to the military,' he said. 'Let them deal with this town's rotten sheriff.'

Hayes looked up at that.

'Your husband was a good man,' he said. 'I'm really sorry for your loss but do as this man says. Let the army send in a town tamer and the sheriff will pay for what he's done, likely at the end of a rope.'

'And you, Hayes' — Blackman looked at the old man, his tone menacing — 'will you pay for your part in helping frame three innocent men, namely me and my pards?'

'I'll face whatever's coming to me and be glad to do so,' the old man said and there was a certain dignity in his voice.

173

'I was powerless to act or I would have, believe me I would have. I will regret it to my last days that I stood by while the sheriff murdered your husband and I'll stand up and say so in any trial. I know it's not much after what's happened but it's all I can do.'

'It's OK,' the widow said, speaking directly to Hayes. 'I understand.'

'I thank you,' Hayes said. 'I truly thank you for those words and please believe me when I say there was nothing I could do to stop the sheriff.'

The widow said nothing but nodded and smiled weakly.

'Then we've done what we came to do,' Slim said. 'Let's get out of here. The sooner we put some dust between us and Hope Springs the more I'll like it.'

'Amen to that,' said Tanner, who was feeling that they'd spent so long here that pretty soon they'd get citizenship.

Suddenly the sound of gunfire filled the air and Hayes was thrown backwards, a grisly third eye opening up in the middle of his forehead. He came to rest at the rear of the stall and slid to the floor, already dead and beyond help. So sudden had the bullet come and ended his life that he had a stunned expression upon his face.

Slim acted immediately and before even clearing leather he pushed the widow to the ground and dived on top of her. Blackman and Tanner returned fire but neither of them had a target as they hid behind a stall.

More gunfire followed and Slim looked up and saw the sheriff through the entrance to the stable. The lawman was crouched down and firing from behind a wagon that someone had placed in the middle of the street. There was no way to get off a clear shot and Slim had to keep under cover as even more bullets powered into the stable walls, sending splinters of wood cascading through the air.

'Come on out,' the sheriff's voice carried from the street outside. 'We know you are in there.'

'You killed Hayes,' Slim shouted. 'You aiming to kill us all?'

'Come out with your hands held high,' the sheriff retorted. 'No one will be harmed.'

Slim knew that was a lie. The sheriff had to kill them all, the widow included, if he was to prevent the truth about the murder of his deputy becoming public knowledge.

The lawman had nothing to lose but everything to gain from killing them.

'Get back there,' Slim told the widow, directing her to the rear of the stable. 'Keep down and make your way over there.'

'But — ' she began but Slim silenced her by holding up a hand.

'You're the key to all this,' Slim said. 'You're the one the sheriff can't leave standing. No one will believe a word me and my pards say without you to back us up. And even if we produce that letter they'll say we forced Hayes to write it. If you die then your husband's killer will never face justice.'

The widow nodded, her eyes wide with a mixture of fear and determination.

'If the way this plays out is that we kill the sheriff,' Slim said, 'then we'll get as far away from here as possible, but you must use that letter and everything you know to clear our names. The sheriff needs you dead, but I very much need you to survive this.'

Again she nodded.

'Good,' Slim said. 'Now get back there and keep under cover.'

Slim sent several shots through the stable doorway while the widow scrambled to the rear of the stable and hid herself down behind a large barrel.

'Can anyone see what we're facing?' Slim shouted.

'I figure the sheriff's got maybe half-a-dozen men with him,' Blackman yelled back, and then had to duck behind the stall as a bullet tore into the woodwork only inches from where his head had been.

'Come out or we'll smoke you out,'

the sheriff yelled.

Slim looked around. He was growing increasingly desperate and couldn't see a way of getting out. If the sheriff sent fire into the stable then it would become a blazing furnace in no time at all. The wooden construction was filled with straw that would ignite easily, as would the building itself, but giving up wasn't an option.

Slim was sure they'd be shot down as soon as they emerged into the open. They would be shot down and the rotten son-of-a-bitch sheriff would be hailed a hero. They had to somehow take the sheriff out and then in the confusion hightail it out, and that was their one and only chance.

'Give us a moment,' Slim shouted back.

'Now,' the sheriff retorted. 'I'm done waiting on varmints like you. This is your last chance to come out.'

Slim didn't answer, but let off a couple of covering shots and quickly made his way to Blackman and Tanner.

There was no more gunfire, only an eerie silence.

Suddenly a lit torch was thrown through the doorway and another quickly followed. Slim watched in horror as the straw upon the floor instantly ignited.

'You two get your horses and get out the back,' Slim said. 'Take the widow with you.'

'There is no back way out,' Blackman said. 'You loco?'

'Use some of the tools to break through,' Slim said. 'Make a back way out.'

'What are you going to do?' Blackman asked.

It was getting difficult to breathe now and the horses in the stalls were beginning to panic as the fire grew and the stable filled with dense smoke.

'I'm going to get the sheriff,' Slim said, and before anyone could argue further he made his way to his horse and pulled the frantic creature from a stall. 'Ride back to the widow's place. I'll meet you there.' He jumped onto his struggling horse. Ahead of them the flames were licking the roof in places, as the building quickly became a furnace.

They all had to get out of here. Get out of here right away.

Blackman and Tanner covered their mouths as best as they could and helped the widow to her feet. Then Tanner went to get the horses while Blackman started beating on the wall with a large hammer. The widow took a look around her and picked up a spade and then she, too, started beating against the wooden wall. The planks of wood splintered immediately and Blackman knew that it would only take a few moments to create a hole big enough for escape.

If only they had a few moments, he thought, as the fire continued to spread at a furious rate.

Tanner joined them, kicking at the splintered planks with his feet.

'Get out of here,' Slim yelled, and spurred his terrified horse towards the front of the stable having to force the beast to run through a section of fire. The horse fought with its rider but Slim kept it under control and then they were emerging from the stable entrance, seeming to appear from out of the flames.

Slim saw the sheriff get to his feet and raise a rifle in his direction. Other men fired from other positions but Slim ignored them and hoped for luck as he aimed, fired and saw the sheriff thrown backwards off his feet, his rifle jerking upwards and firing widely into the sky.

'Sombitch',' Slim said, as he saw the sheriff clutching at the thick bloodstain that was spreading across the centre of his chest.

Within seconds he was dead.

That was one killing Slim wouldn't be losing sleep over.

Slim spurred his horse harder and sent it off galloping up the main street. He kept low in the saddle so he would present less of a target. Red-hot lead creased the air above him as he spurred the terrified horse into an even faster gallop. He reached the end of the main street and then took his horse into a

12

'Got them,' Baxter said, and dropped the telescope from his eye. He handed it to the deputy who was beside him on the rise that looked down into the Black Valleys.

Rawlings lifted the telescope to his right eye, closed his left, and looked through it.

There, a few miles distant, he could see the men they had been chasing for so many miles. The telescope, actually a riflesight, didn't have enough magnification to pick out any real detail of the distant riders, but the deputy could see there were three of them. However, as he watched, it became clear that the third man, the one on the rear horse, was seated awkwardly and appeared to be lying out rigid in the saddle. It was difficult to say with any certainty since all he could really make out through the 'scope were shapes, but the deputy suddenly realized that this third man wasn't a man at all but rather the mummified corpse of Slim McCord.

It had to be. It was the only explanation.

'How far ahead are they?' the deputy asked, handing the telescope back to Baxter.

'A few miles,' the tracker said, and slid the sight into his tunic. 'We've got to get down into the valley, though. That will take time, but I reckon that with hard riding we could catch up with them by sundown or thereabouts. Depends if they notice us and speed up.'

'They ain't seen us yet,' Rawlings said. Without the telescope the distant riders were nothing more than black spots and not really visible at all, so it was a given that they themselves were invisible to the outlaws.

'No,' Baxter agreed. 'Not yet they ain't.'

'I figure the third rider's our missing

corpse,' the deputy said.

'Yep,' Baxter replied. That was pretty much the way he figured it too.

'Why would anyone steal a corpse?' Rawlings asked. 'Why not just get the hell away with the money? That was a big haul they took, the biggest I've ever heard tell of.'

'A fortune,' Baxter agreed. 'Enough to last a man for several lifetimes.'

'But why steal that damn mummified outlaw? What has that corpse got to do with any of this?'

'Men do strange things,' Baxter said.

'But a corpse,' the deputy retorted. 'What possible use could a corpse be to them?'

'Maybe he's in charge,' Baxter said with a grim smile and spat into the dirt.

'Who are these men?' Rawlings asked, thoughtfully. He neither expected nor received an answer from the tracker.

The deputy turned so as to face the other four members of the posse. It had been a long exhausting ride and the men were lagging, feeling the strain of the miles they had covered. The deputy knew that the time had come for a talk with them. They were close to catching up with their quarry and they needed a little inspiration just about now.

'We've spotted them,' Rawlings said and found that he immediately had the attention of his posse.

The men were not professional lawmen, they were townsfolk, family men who had been drafted into the posse and had only served out of a sense of duty to their town. Of course they had been keen at first, eager even to get on the trail of the men who had robbed the town bank, but by now they were tired, missing both their families and the home comforts provided by such. The cold realization that this was not going to be the brief adventure they had hoped was now apparent to each and every one of them.

The deputy knew from past experience that it was difficult to motivate tired men, doubly so with those who were undisciplined and untrained, and that once they had reached a certain point of despair there was no turning things around.

'A day, two at the most,' he said. 'And we should be starting back with the men who robbed our bank. They'll swing for their crimes and it is all thanks to you men. When we return to town with the stolen monies you men will have earned the gratitude of each and every citizen in Possum Creek.'

There were murmurs amongst the men but little more. If the deputy had been expecting cheers then he wasn't getting any, but he did feel that the news their quarry had at last been spotted had lifted their spirits — if only slightly.

'We ride out in a few minutes,' he concluded. 'Get yourselves ready, check your rigs because we'll be riding hard to run these men down.' A few cheers would not have gone amiss at this point, but at least the men responded by grudgingly going to their respective horses and ensuring they were ready for the ride. They had already ridden through the night and had only been resting a few minutes so the fact that they were moving at all was something to be grateful for.

If there was one consolation in all this, the deputy figured, no matter how fatigued his men were the two outlaws would be just as tired, if not more so.

'The men are getting ready,' Rawlings said to Baxter. The tracker was standing perfectly still, his attention seemingly focused on the far horizon. 'We'll pull out momentarily.'

Baxter nodded, said nothing.

Rawlings turned away and went to his own horse. The tracker was indeed a strange one, the deputy reflected. He seemed to be alone even when surrounded, as he was now, by others. A difficult man to get to know, he was even harder to like, but the deputy didn't pay it too much mind, since Baxter was a damn fine tracker, quite probably the best in the business. He had, so it was said, helped the army in tracking down a band of hostile Apaches who had evaded attempts to run them down for the best part of a decade. Any man who could track an Apache could likely track a snowflake in a storm and the deputy was glad to have him along. It was due to Baxter that they had gotten as far as they had and already they had tracked the outlaws through some inhospitable territory. Not once during the night ride had the man's eagle eyes lost sight of tracks that most men wouldn't be able to see during the brightest of days.

Rawlings mounted his horse and spun the beast around.

'Come on, men,' he shouted. 'We'll be riding through the night again if need be, so let's make the best of the daylight.'

Baxter was already mounted and he spurred his horse onwards, while Rawlings took up position beside him with the rest of the posse following up behind. It was the formation the tracker insisted on, everyone was to stay directly behind him, the horses to follow the line he set. That way, he claimed, the tracks he followed would not be compromised by the tracks of men who couldn't really see what they were following, where they were going.

13

Day had become night and once more returned before Blackman and Tanner realized the posse was so close.

Blackman saw the dust on the distant horizon and looked at it for several minutes before understanding what it meant. The dust was being thrown into the air by a band of riders coming through the valley. They were moving fast, likely as fast as their horses could carry them.

'Posse,' he said, pointing and Tanner came and stood beside him.

'Shit,' Tanner said.

'Come on.' Blackman quickly made his way to the horses. 'We need to get out of here.' He grabbed the reins of the horse carrying Slim's remains and made sure it was tied tightly to the pommel of his saddle. They were going to be moving faster than they had for the entire ride, and the horses would need to gallop at the best of their ability.

'How many you figure?' Tanner asked, jumping into his saddle with an agility that belied his age.

Blackman looked back, squinting at the dust cloud.

'Difficult to say,' he said. 'Anywhere between five and ten men I'd say.'

'That's what I figure.'

Blackman's face clouded over with worry.

They had gone so far along the trail without any incident other than the Indian attack, that he had dared to believe they were safe from any pursuing law. Now though it was evident that this was not the case: the law was very much after them.

'Let's ride,' he said, and spurred his horse into a gallop. The horse behind was startled by the sudden tightening of the reins and held back for a second; almost sending Blackman falling from the saddle, but it soon went with the horse in front when it realized it had no choice.

'Which way?' Tanner shouted, holding his horse level with Blackman's, which wasn't easy since the beast wanted to spurt ahead and without the burden of having another horse tied to it, Tanner's mount was much faster.

'Up into the hills,' Blackman said. 'The valley opens up a little further on and we can maybe shake them off there.'

'Or make a stand,' Tanner shouted back. There would be places in the valleys where they could hide out and more easily defend themselves against greater numbers.

'If it comes to it,' Blackman said. 'If it comes to it.'

The ground elevated sharply and Blackman and Tanner had to struggle with their horses as they started up a steep rise that went up into the rocks that ran clean out of the valley. It was a far more difficult trail than sticking to the valley floor but the old outlaws felt that it offered the best chance of escape. It was hard, often impossible, to track anyone over rock and the men were hoping the posse would continue along the valley floor.

Blackman knew they would be invisible to the posse when they rounded the bend in the rocks, and so he cast a glance over his shoulder, and although the posse were still little more than a dust cloud on the horizon it was plain to see that they were gaining on them.

Maybe I am too old for this, Blackman thought, and dug his spurs in harder. His horse let out a snort and then increased its speed, the horse behind having to pick up to the same pace.

They had covered maybe a mile before they allowed their horses to slow their speed. The ground beneath them, a mixture of sand and clay, was soft and made the trail ponderous for the horses and ahead of them lay some of the most hazardous terrain in the world, at least the bits of the world the two men were familiar with.

Blackman looked behind them and smiled when he saw no sign of the posse.

'I've an idea,' he said.

'Let's hear it,' Tanner said, turning in his saddle.

'We'll tie Slim back up behind me,' Blackman said. 'Send the other horse off in the opposite direction. Maybe the posse will split up to follow both trails.'

'Maybe,' Tanner said, but didn't think that at all likely. Sooner or later, he knew, the posse would catch up with them.

And what then?

A shoot out?

The thought of a shoot out was not something that either man relished, but they knew deep down that it might prove inevitable. They didn't want to kill anyone and they certainly didn't want to get killed themselves, but all the same they knew that if it came to it, they would be forced to play their hands. They would never surrender; they were both far too old to go back to jail and had known the risks when they'd pulled the robbery. The same risks were always there, sometimes it came to shooting and sometimes it didn't, but the possibility was always there.

'Here,' Blackman said, pulling the horses to a stop. 'We'll send Slim's horse galloping off yonder. We scare it enough and it won't stop running till it can't run no more.'

'Redneck peckerwood,' Tanner spat into the dust and then pulled his own horse to a sudden halt. He jumped from the saddle in order to help Blackman get Slim from one horse and onto the other.

The two men untied Slim and manhandled him from the saddle. They lay him down on the ground while they transferred the sack of money from Blackman's horse and onto Tanner's. They didn't want to weigh one horse down with too much weight since both men needed as much stamina and speed from their mounts as was possible. Then they lifted Slim onto Blackman's horse and although there was no real weight to the mummified outlaw, it was still an arduous task. Slim was stiff, rigid, and not at all pliable.

It took some time to get the body onto the horse.

'Remember that time we were down in Texas?' Blackman said, as he secured the last strap to Slim's body. 'When we pulled off that stage robbery in Fort Worth?'

'Hell of a time to reminisce,' Tanner said, and led the spare horse down the trail a little, before whipping the beast on the rump with the flat of his hand, and screaming out a blood curdling yell.

The horse immediately set off towards the east.

Blackman was now in his own saddle, seated behind Slim's body, which was virtually sitting upright in the saddle. The dead outlaw's legs stretched out behind Blackman, which made riding difficult but there was no other way. They were not going to dump the body of their old friend out here. That, Blackman knew, was the wise thing to do, what with the posse in pursuit an' all, but the old outlaw would not consider it.

It was just not the sort of thing a man could do to a friend: even a dead friend.

'We're running out of time,' Tanner said, 'and you want to waste it with a trip down Memory Lane.'

'No,' Blackman said. 'I'm not making idle chitter-chatter. Remember that posse they sent after us? When we robbed that stage near Fort Worth they sent a posse after us. Remember that posse?'

Tanner looked at his old friend. He had a vague memory of the posse being particularly difficult to shake, but other than that there was nothing that stuck in his mind.

'I remember,' he said.

'They were able to track us over

rock,' Blackman pointed out. 'Followed us all the way through the badlands.'

'So?'

'And out onto the plains beyond,' Blackman continued. 'Slim had us burn the grass behind us and yet they still followed us. Not once losing our trail until we gave them the slip along the coastline and that was by pure luck.'

Tanner shrugged, said nothing but his expression spoke a volume of cuss words.

'They remind me of this posse now,' Blackman said.

'What's the point?' Tanner asked. 'You suggesting that this here posse is the very same one?'

'Maybe,' Blackman said.

'Well,' Tanner spat. 'That just isn't possible. We were young then but those fellas in the posse were all whiskered and grey. They'd all be dead by now, long dead.'

Blackman shrugged his shoulders. He knew that was true, but sometimes he forgot just how old they had become and lost track of the passage of time. There were times when twenty years ago felt like yesterday, and others when the world he had grown up in became a distant, truly ancient speck on the corner of memory.

'Don't seem right that a man should come up against such a posse twice in one lifetime,' he said.

'Redneck peckerwood,' Tanner said and set his horse off galloping west.

'Come on then, Slim,' Blackman said and set off after his pard.

Slim, of course, said nothing but stared straight ahead.

14

Night had once again fallen and made further progress difficult.

'We need to stop,' Rawlings said, pulling on the reins of his horse and holding up a hand to stop the men behind him.

'We're close now,' Baxter said. 'I reckon in a few hours we'd be upon them.'

'The horses ain't got a few hours in them,' Rawlings said, and dismounted. He loosened his saddle straps and grabbed his canteen. He took a mouthful of water and wiped his mouth with the back of a hand. 'We'll rest up for a little while. Ride back out before dawn.'

'Guess so,' Baxter said grudgingly, and climbed from his own horse. Now that they were so close, he felt as if he could smell the men they were chasing.

He had their scent and was eager to run them down.

A few hours ago, just before dusk they had once again spotted the men through the telescope. This time the distance between them had not been so great and they had been able to pick out a lot of detail. They could see the mummified outlaw clearly and could also pick out some other features of the man who rode double with the dead man. He looked to be an old man, as did the other one who followed behind him. They had wondered what had happened to the third horse, but Baxter suggested they had turned it free, hoping to create a false trail, which, he said, was an old trick and not one he'd likely fall for.

'Four hours, men,' Rawlings yelled. 'See to your horses and then get some shut-eye. Tomorrow we catch them.'

The lawman truly believed that, he realized, as he sat himself down on the hard ground and took his makings from his shirt pocket. When this was all over, he promised himself, he'd spend a full day in bed.

★   ★   ★

'You ain't got a single idea where we are,' Tanner insisted.

'I know where we are,' Blackman said.

The two men were on foot now, leading their horses behind them. The ground beneath their feet was uneven and it was too dark to ride. There was a lot of cloud in the night sky through which the moonlight was filtered.

'Well, if that's true,' Tanner said, 'Then what's that noise I can hear?'

Blackman said nothing. He could hear the sound himself and knew what it meant, but he also knew that they shouldn't be hearing a sound like that. Not for some miles yet.

'It's a river,' Tanner said. 'A big rushing river. I reckon it's running through that canyon yonder.' It was difficult to tell just how close they were to the river, since sound had an odd way of travelling at night, but there was no mistaking the noise of those raging torrents.

Blackman nodded, but once again said nothing. He kept his attention on the narrow mountain trail they were negotiating.

'If we're where you say we are there shouldn't be no river.' Tanner stopped walking, felt the reins go slack as his horse immediately stopped with him. He reached into his shirt and took out his makings, rolling himself a cigarette. 'You've gone and got us lost and we don't know what we'll find around the next bend.'

Blackman stopped, spun on his feet. He gave Slim a knowing look as if his long dead friend would commiserate with him, and then glared at Tanner.

'Quit bellyaching,' he said. 'You're getting clucky in your old age.'

Tanner shook his head, looking at his old friend with a dumbfounded realization that he may very well have lost his mind.

'We were doing OK,' he said.

'Nothing special, but getting from day to day with as little effort as possible and you had to louse it all up with this madness.'

'We were drifting,' Blackman said. 'We'd been drifting for years. That ain't living.'

'Let's rob a bank, you said. Let's take Slim with us, you said.' The disagreement was in danger of turning into a full-blown argument and Tanner was not going to back down. 'Now look at us — we're dragging a corpse around with us, we're hopelessly lost and we've got a posse so close that they could reach out and grab us.'

'We're also rich,' Blackman reminded his friend, unable to think of anything else to say.

Tanner laughed at that, couldn't help himself and he went right on laughing for several moments.

'Loco redneck peckerwood,' he said finally and drew the last from his quirly before flicking it away into the darkness. He watched the glowing ember until it suddenly blinked out of existence.

'We should keep moving,' Blackman said after a moment, during which he stared into the darkness, trying to figure out exactly where they were. 'We'll walk a'ways and then ride a'ways. Just as long as we keep moving.'

'Yeah,' Tanner nodded. 'Seems we always gotta keep on moving.'

The two old men continued climbing the mountain trail. The third man, if he could be called a man at all, remained silent in the saddle as his two old pards took him further along the journey that had started long before his death.

★　★　★

Dawn was still brand new when the first gunshot rang out.

A second and then a third followed it before Tanner found the ground rushing to meet him as he was thrown forwards from his horse. He hit the ground hard, and immediately looked back to see his horse dead on the ground, a thick mess of blood around the wound in the side of its head.

'Damn.' Tanner spat and noticed the posse coming up the trail. There were six of them and they were all shooting as they coaxed as much speed as was possible out of their exhausted horses. He cleared leather and sent off a shot in the general direction of the posse while he tried to get to his feet.

Blackman looked back and saw Tanner on the ground. He immediately pulled his horse to a stop, spun it around and galloped back to Tanner.

'Get up,' Blackman said, holding out a hand for Tanner to grab.

Tanner shot at the posse again and then grabbed his friend's hand and jumped onto the back of the horse. There were now three of them, including Slim's remains, on the frightened horse and Blackman dug his spurs in to get the beast galloping back up the trail.

'The money,' Tanner said. 'We've left the money behind.'

'Shit,' Blackman said, as a bullet went over his head. It had been so close that he could feel the heat of it upon his scalp.

'The money,' Tanner repeated. He again sent off several shots in the direction of the posse, hoping at the very least to slow them down.

'You want to go back for it?'

'Hell, no!' Tanner said, as a slug passed through the flair of his left pants leg but miraculously missed his flesh.

After all they had been through it should end like this, Blackman thought, as he tried to get his horse to gain a little speed. All that money, a fortune beyond their wildest dreams was now lost to them and all they had for their troubles was the remains of their oldest friend.

'Send some heat their way,' Blackman yelled. It was not as if he could fire at the posse, not with the two men, one dead and the other very much alive, on the horse with him.

Tanner did so, noticing that there

were only three members of the posse in pursuit. The others must have stayed with the money. He sent his slugs wide, not that he could hit any of the pursuing men in any case as he was thrown about in the saddle.

Blackman took his horse around another bend and found that they had run out of trail. All that lay ahead of them was a cliff face with a sheer drop to the raging river below. He pulled the horse to a stop and, dismounting, immediately started to untie Slim from the horse before Tanner had even climbed down.

Tanner jumped from the horse, crouched down and fired back at the posse who had also dismounted and were taking up positions behind the rocks which provided natural cover. Once they had Slim from the horse Blackman slapped the beast's rump, sending it galloping back down the trail towards the posse. This afforded them a few seconds as the posse members had to avoid the terrified horse which could have thrown them over the cliff edge to their certain death below.

'There,' Blackman shouted and started dragging Slim's body behind a large rock. Tanner let off two more shots and then followed them, diving down behind the rock and feeling his hat torn from his head as a slug found it.

Blackman suddenly stood up, fired three times and then ducked back down behind the rock. They were at the edge of the rock face and he glanced down at the rushing water below.

'Now what?' Tanner yelled. Behind them they had the well-armed posse and in front of them lay the certain death of a fall into the icy waters of the fierce river below.

'Surrendering seems the only option,' Blackman said, as a slug hit the rock and sent dust into his face.

'Not likely,' Tanner said, and sent off another shot at the posse. 'I'm too old to go back to jail. I ain't going to die in jail.'

'Then we'll die here,' Blackman said.

'Don't much relish that either,' Tanner said. 'But I ain't going to give up.'

Blackman looked down to the river below them. He wasn't sure how far the drop was, but it was considerable and the chances were if they tried it they would get cut to pieces by the jagged rocks that protruded from the cliff face.

'We could jump,' he suggested.

Tanner looked down.

'Not likely,' he said.

'It's our only chance,' Blackman said. 'We may make it and if we don't it'll be better than dying here or rotting in some prison.'

Again Tanner glanced down at the river.

'I ain't jumping,' he said.

'The three of us,' Blackman said. 'We'll go over together.'

Tanner looked at Slim's remains lying between them.

'He's already dead,' he said, as several bullets chipped away at the rock they hid behind. 'And we'll be too if we jump.'

'We die here,' Blackman said, 'or take our chances down there.'

'Loco redneck peckerwood,' Tanner retorted and shot back at the posse. He couldn't get a clear shot at any of the men since they had too much natural cover. He knew they were beat and although he and Blackman were well concealed themselves all the posse would have to do would be to keep them pinned down until starvation finally drove them out.

Blackman stood up, lifting Slim with him and holding his dead friend's body around the waist.

'I'm gonna jump,' he said, as another slug went zipping above his head.

'You're loco,' Tanner snapped back, and let off another shot.

'It's our only chance.' Blackman said.

'It ain't no chance.' Tanner again fired at the posse.

'Slim will protect us,' Blackman said.

Tanner sighed and then he also stood up. He too placed an arm around Slim's waist. 'Let's do it,' he said.

'On the count of three,' Blackman said.

Tanner gulped, nodded.

'One, two, three,' Blackman yelled, and then the two men suddenly stepped out into thin air, taking the body of their oldest friend with them.

★ ★ ★

Yesteryear

'I don't know how I can thank you,' the widow said. 'The three of you.'

'You just clear our name with the law,' Slim said. 'That'll be thanks enough.'

Immediately following the incident at the livery stable they had ridden directly to the widow's place, where they had decided to accompany her to the army outpost.

Jake, the man who had been with the family a long time, first serving her grandfather, protested. He had been with the Conner clan since long before the emancipation declaration had made him a free man, and then decided to stay on because the Conners were the closest thing he had to a family of his own.

The widow was once again firm. She convinced Jake to stay with the children while she took the letter to the army, told them her story so that any accomplices of the sheriff could be rounded up to face justice and the names of Slim McCord and his companions be cleared of the murder of her husband.

'I will,' she said and looked down at the small fort, which acted as an army outpost.

'Reckon you'll be safe enough from here on your own,' Slim said. 'And me and the boys would like to disappear before the army takes to questioning us.'

The widow nodded, said once more, 'Thank you.'

'Pleasure,' Slim said, and immediately sent his horse off galloping in the opposite direction, Blackman and Tanner following behind him.

15

Blackman swallowed a mouthful of water and gasped for air as he broke through the surface of the river. The currents were strong and once more he found himself dragged under before again breaking the surface.

'Give me your hand. Grab hold.'

Blackman heard Tanner's yells above the roar of the water.

Blackman looked to his left and saw Tanner being carried downriver.

Slim was floating in front of him with Tanner holding on to the dead outlaw's body as if he were some kind of float.

'Come on,' Tanner yelled, and swallowed a mouthful of water himself. He cursed and spat it out.

Blackman reached out for Tanner's hand, but missed, and once again he was dragged down beneath the surface. He emerged, coughing and spluttering and then with an almighty surge of effort he reached out and found Tanner's hand. He kicked his legs against the pull of the water and managed to get himself across and then he too gripped onto Slim's body, which kept them afloat.

The sawdust and whatnot that the undertaker had used to stuff Slim had turned the man's corpse into a useful makeshift raft.

The two men were carried down-river, the body of their long dead friend keeping them from drowning in the icy cold depths of the river.

Once again Slim had saved them.

* * *

They were carried for several miles before they reached calmer waters and managed to kick themselves ashore. The two men, Slim on the ground between them, lay on the river-bank for some time while they caught their breath.

'I guess that's it,' Blackman said and managed to get to his feet. 'It's over.

The posse ain't gonna be able to follow us now.'

Tanner nodded and reached into his pocket for his makings but they were soaked beyond use. In disgust he tossed them onto the ground.

'This is as good a place as any,' Blackman said.

'What are you talking about now?' Tanner asked. He was finding it hard to take in all that had happened to them. They had started out the day as rich men with a life of luxury ahead of them, and now, merely hours later, they were once again penniless and on the lam. Still, he supposed, it was some comfort that they had shaken off that damn posse.

'To bury Slim,' Blackman said.

'I guess so,' Tanner replied.

The men looked around and both of them considered the small rise above the river-bank to be a likely place for a burial. A grave dug there would get the morning sun and there was nothing more peaceful sounding than the gentle flow of the river.

It was a suitable resting place for their old friend.

Blackman reached into his shirt pocket and pulled out the three dollar bills he had picked up from the floor in the bank. He looked at the money for a moment and then smiled and handed one to Tanner, and bent and popped one into Slim's pocket. The remaining bill he placed back into his own pocket.

Tanner looked at Blackman.

'We didn't lose all the money then,' he said with a wry smile.

'That's our total haul shared out equal,' Blackman said. 'Between you, Slim and me.'

'Loco, redneck peckerwood,' Tanner said.

'Just like old times,' Blackman smiled.

'Loco, redneck peckerwood,' Tanner repeated and looked around for something they could use as makeshift spades.

They had a grave to dig.

16

A week later the following article, credited to the byline G.M. Dobbs appeared in the *Possum Creek Chronicle*.

THE GREAT MYSTERY OF SLIM MCCORD

It is thanks to the bravery and skill of Deputy Rawlings and his posse that the incredible haul stolen from the town bank was recovered. However, despite the fast action of the posse, for which the town will be forever grateful, the identities and whereabouts of the bandits remain unknown. At the time of the robbery the town bank was holding large sums of government monies intended for tribal payouts, and a government spokesman recently commended the actions of the deputy and his posse in averting terrible consequences by recovering the sum stolen by the unknown bandits.

The most bizarre aspect to the robbery is that the bandits seemed to have also stolen the mummified remains of notorious outlaw, Slim McCord, from a travelling carnival show where it was a popular, if rather gruesome exhibit. Unlike the money, the body is yet to be recovered and this is provoking much fanciful speculation. One story heard in the saloons of Possum Creek is that the outlaw returned to life and engineered the bank robbery himself, whilst another equally outlandish story is that the two men seen riding with McCord were actually ghosts of his old gang members. These outlandish claims are given credence by the most perplexing mystery of how the bank was entered in the first place. There were no signs of a forced entry and the bank was securely locked when the manager arrived to open for business the morning following the robbery.

'There was something odd about that corpse,' Thomas Ryder, owner of the travelling carnival, which owned the remains of Slim McCord, told the *Chronicle*. 'There have been so many strange happenings since I bought him, and I wouldn't be surprised if he had returned from the grave and pulled off the robbery.'

The truth may never be fully known but the one thing that is certain is that the mystery of Slim McCord will be the subject of wild conversation for considerable time to come.

THE END